Pennies
from
Heaven

Pennies from Heaven

a romance

JENNIFER ROSE

Copyright © 1984 by Jennifer Rose

Cover design by Kat JK Lee

ISBN: 978-1-5040-2040-4

Distributed in 2015 by Open Road Distribution
345 Hudson Street
New York, NY 10014
www.openroadmedia.com

for Millie and Norm, a real-life romance

Acknowledgments

Grazie mille to Richard Anderson for his lyrical recollections of life in Venice, and to Kent Mockler and Sherri Duprey for making the connection.

Carolyn and Roger Tyndall, publishers of *The Contest News-Letter*, provided valuable insiders' information about contests and sweepstakes.

Any errors are, of course, my own.

Pennies
from
Heaven

Let us then understand at once that change or variety is as much a necessity to the human heart and brain in buildings as in books; that there is no merit, though there is some occasional use, in monotony; and that we must no more expect to derive either pleasure or profit from an architecture whose ornaments are of one pattern, and whose pillars are of one proportion, than we should out of a universe in which the clouds were all of one shape, and the trees all of one size.

—John Ruskin
The Stones of Venice

Chapter 1

MADELINE WHELAN LOVED CLARK WHELAN. She'd engraved the message in cement on the sidewalk in front of their modest white two-story house: MW xxx CW.

Ask her why, and she would probably shrug her shoulders and give you a puzzled grin. How not to love Clark? He just happened to be the kindest, warmest, most honorable man she'd ever met. The handsomest and sexiest, too. There was nothing *not* to love about him.

Even his occasional sudden moodiness added to his appeal. He got moody because he took life seriously. Maddy had no patience with people who took themselves seriously, but she had no respect for people who refused to take life seriously.

Maddy loved Clark and their eight-year-old twin daughters and, in varying degrees, most of the people she encountered in the course of her days. And Maddy hated . . . umbrellas.

Umbrellas cluttered the hands. They threatened the eyes. (At five feet ten and a half inches Maddy found herself at eye level with most other women's spokes.) Cheap umbrellas snapped in the first good gust, and expensive ones got lost.

Above all other flaws, umbrellas were unromantic. In *Breakfast at*

Tiffany's, one of Maddy's favorite movies, Audrey Hepburn revealed the vulnerable state of her heart by letting the rain drench her hair. An umbrella would have ruined the scene and diminished the power of the movie.

Maddy hated umbrellas, but she didn't want to meet Clark with her hair a soggy mess. She knew she was striking, and she knew Clark thought her beautiful; she also knew she wasn't Audrey Hepburn.

She had that height, and she had strong, bold features. Her eyebrows were broad stripes, rivaled in intensity by lashes so thick she didn't dare wear mascara. Her nose had an all-American tilt, but it was a real nose, a grown-up nose, not a girlish pug. She had the sort of full lips that looked perpetually kiss-swollen; it had taken her well into her teens to be comfortable with those lips, to dare to gloss them. Her chin was a ship of state, sailing fearlessly into troubled waters, smoothing the waves.

All in all, hers was a face that needed brilliant, bouncy hair as a frame and counterweight. Dry hair.

Besides, Clark had something of an obsession with her hair. After nearly ten years of marriage, he claimed he was still finding new earth tones sparking the dominant copper. Umber, amber, ocher, he liked to recite, reminding Maddy of childhood troves of crayons with magical names. The no-nonsense lights at the Olympus Diner, where she was meeting Clark for lunch, might not do much for her complexion or anyone else's, but they would make her hair dance and shimmer and maybe yield a new color.

If she kept it dry.

She stared out the kitchen window, watching the rain stream down on the driveway. Some of the drops did a little jig, dancing back up into the air, or was that a trick played on the eye? Others gathered into pools—where the potholes were, Maddy guessed. Repaving the driveway was on what the Whelans called The List. Maddy shrugged cheerfully. What did a few potholes matter?

Anyway, one of these days she was going to win a sweepstakes or a jingle contest or a bake-off. Pennies would fall from heaven the way the rain was falling today. Then everything on The List would get done.

Or maybe she'd never win anything and The List would just keep growing. She would still count herself the luckiest woman.

She had Clark. She had the twins, the most enchanting eight-year-old girls anyone could hope for. They were all healthy, thank the Lord. She and Clark and the girls had what the world was panting and clawing for: happiness. Because they didn't want too much, they had everything.

She would wear a hat, Maddy decided. Hats made her feel less free, but she didn't positively dislike them, the way she did umbrellas.

Then again, her hat situation wasn't exactly terrific. The red hat that matched her slicker had been used once too often as a fire fighter's headgear in the twins' imaginative games. As for the formerly raffish cap that matched her trench coat: It had a big egg-shaped stain on it—some kind of oil, they'd said at Clem's Cwik Cleaners, giving up. Come to think of it, her trench coat was stained, too. Getting new rain gear for Maddy was on The List, somewhere between reframing the precious photograph of Clark's paternal grandparents and replacing the battered wicker furniture on the screened-in porch.

With a grin and a shrug Maddy banished The List from her thoughts. If it weren't for Clark, she'd wear the red slicker hat today and every rainy day until it actually fell apart. But Clark was as vain on her behalf as he was free of vanity on his own.

He wasn't label-conscious, like so much of the world around them, but he got upset if Maddy wore anything he considered shabby. The one dress he'd ever asked her to return to a shop was a pre-washed denim prairie number that he said looked as though it had been dragged kicking and screaming through the dust into the last frontier. No shabby-as-chic for Clark!

Maddy took out a pristine red and silver Italian silk scarf, folded it—as she always did—to obscure the designer's signature, put it over her head, and tied it behind her neck, model style. Impulsively she added a pair of small sterling-silver hoop earrings Clark had given her one Christmas.

She'd do very nicely, the mirror reported.

As she pulled the Volkswagen Beetle into the rainswept parking lot in front of the Olympus Diner, she saw Clark's van, parked between a red MG with Connecticut plates and a vintage Ford station wagon with real wooden panels. She glanced at her watch, and her heart quickened with joy. *She* wasn't late; *he* had come early. Oh, she was luckier than lucky, married to a man so eager to see her a mere four hours after breakfast.

Clark rose with unforced gallantry as Maddy approached their favorite booth. "Hello, darling." His lips brushed hers, then came back and lingered for an instant. He helped her out of her slicker and hung it from the hook they shared with the adjoining booth. "No, leave it on," he said as she reached behind her neck to untie the red and silver scarf. "You look like a beautiful gypsy. Like a runaway baroness trying to disguise herself as a gypsy. Very spicy."

Maddy grinned. "For a man with big shoulders, you have a nice imagination. Of course, the whole point of the scarf was to preserve my hair so you could ogle it during lunch." She left the scarf where it was.

"Ogle, do I?" Clark pushed aside a red plastic tomato-shaped ketchup dispenser and took Maddy's hand. "Can a man ogle his own wife?"

"*You* can, thank heaven," she said.

She settled back on the cracked maroon banquette, pleasure traveling up her back and making her shoulders feel light. Her lunches with Clark had a special quality. Around them the eternal buzz of the Olympus rose and fell: heavy plates and cutlery clattering against formica; Dilly, the waitress, calling out orders in dinerspeak. "Adam and Eve on a raft. Stretch two." But Maddy and Clark always spun their own world around them, independent of time and place.

Maddy picked up the menu, though she knew it by heart, down to the daily specials. If this was Thursday, there had to be corned beef hash. She loved homemade hash, and she had the kind of metabolism that let her eat the calorie-loaded dishes the diet-conscious world had to pass up.

"Hash for me," she said to Clark. He liked to give her order to the waiter or waitress whenever they ate out, and she didn't mind, though her more determined feminist friends would have scolded her. She thought it was sweet of him, in fact. "Two poached eggs. Rye toast. Let's hope none of my customers sees me."

Maddy distributed the Mother Earth line of vitamins, minerals, natural cosmetics, and non-toxic household cleaners; and she had a feeling she wasn't supposed to be seen eating saturated fat. She'd had homemade low-fat yogurt and seven-grain muffins for breakfast, as virtue would have it, but who would know? Oh, well. Her customers were more likely to lunch at the Honeydale Lawn Club than at the Olympus Diner.

Dilly nodded her kind, round face approvingly, though, when Clark gave her their order. "Hash takes whiskey down," she called out over her shoulder. "BLT, hold the mayo. Draw two," she added, knowing without being told that Maddy and Clark both wanted coffee.

Maddy gave a little hum of appreciation as the coffee arrived, dark and slightly oily in thick white mugs. "Love that caffeine," she said contentedly as the first jolt hit her.

"You're a marvelously contradictory woman. Do you know that?" Clark's gray eyes gleamed. "Preaching the joys of yogurt one minute, caffeine the next."

"A hypocrite, do you mean?" Maddy's voice was light, but she needed to ask the question.

Clark shook his head emphatically. "No, my heart. Not you. Never. You have a giant-size soul, that's all. Room for everything." His eyes danced appreciatively over her face, then narrowed suddenly, the gleaming gray turning smoky. "Maddy, why don't you buy some new rain stuff this afternoon? Coat, hat, boots, the works."

The broad planes of his face took on a tautness, as if he were fighting to keep from showing physical pain. Maddy felt the pleasure being siphoned out of her. She knew the signs all too well. Clark was worrying about money, hating not having more, thinking she must be secretly miserable about the material constrictions of their life.

"Hey," she said softly. Her fingers made a playground of his hand. "One minute you tell me you love what I'm wearing, and the next you want me to replace it. I may be contradictory, but you're downright confounding."

"You're so damn gorgeous." Clark paid the compliment as if he half regretted the truth behind it. "You should be wearing silk down to your toes. Eating lobster salad and drinking champagne."

Maddy looked him straight in the eyes. "I don't mind our not having much money, and you know it. I just mind your minding. Anyway, I don't like lobster. And champagne tickles my nose." She took a defiant sip of coffee.

"Don't humor me," Clark said darkly.

"Humor you! I could swat you." Maddy set her mug down with punishing force. "I guess this is what I deserve for being so self-congratulatory," she went on, her mouth straining into a wry grin. "You know what I was thinking just before I left the house? How lucky we are. Not in spite of being broke; maybe because of it. So many people we know are obsessed with *things*. Labels. Designer jeans, designer cars, designer water. Where to get the best croissant in Honeydale. Somehow we escaped."

"Then how come you keep entering those contests?" Clark asked. "Talking about blue-sky money, buying us everything we ever wanted?"

Dilly set plates down in front of them. "Enjoy," she said. "Hot up your coffee?"

"Please, Dilly." Looking at Clark through a plume of steam, Maddy slowly shook her head. "Clark Whelan, you know perfectly well why I enter those contests. For the fun of it. And because I'm a born competitor, and I'm not particularly eager to compete with you or the girls." A real smile curved her lips. "If I weren't so competitive, I wouldn't have won you."

"What do you mean? You were head of the cheerleading squad. Almost as gorgeous then as you are now." The light seeping back into his eyes, he said, "You were the prize."

Maddy's fork hovered over her hash. "Don't be modest. I can't bear it. You were captain of the football team. You could have had any girl you wanted, and you know it."

"I guess you're right," Clark said. "I did get every girl I wanted. You."

It was true, Maddy knew; her favorite truth. She and Clark had needed scarcely more than a glance to fall totally, irrevocably in love. Even the grownups in their lives had respected their attachment. When they'd announced their decision to marry the day after their high school graduation, no one had urged them to wait and test the waters.

It had to be Clark for Maddy; it had to be Maddy for Clark. She'd wanted the words "forsaking all others" stricken from the marriage ceremony; the phrase seemed superfluous and insulting. For the Whelans there *were* no others.

Dilly stopped at their booth, hands on hips that looked like too many desserts. "Something wrong with that sandwich, hon?" She glared at Clark. "You haven't touched it."

"I'm sure it's fine, Dilly. I'm just too much in love to eat."

"Oh, boy," Dilly snorted. "I'll go tell the chef there's enough corn out here to make a ten-gallon pot of chowder."

"You missed your calling. You should have been a nanny." With an exaggerated sigh of resignation, Clark bit into his sandwich. "Delicious."

"You're sweet," Maddy murmured as Dilly moved on, satisfied. "You know how to make people feel good."

"That's the beautiful part of being a cornball."

"You're not corny," Maddy said. "Just an old-fashioned romantic." She eyed him appraisingly, a smile on her lips. "Well, maybe a little bit corny. But on you it looks good."

It was true, she thought. His powerful body was the perfect foil for courtly gestures. The keen intelligence illuminating his eyes offset his softer sentiments and kept them from being mere mush. What might have been false or weak in a lesser man rang true and strong in Clark. Even at the Olympus Diner, dressed in a blue Oxford cloth shirt with rolled-up sleeves and a pair of old chinos, he reminded her of the urbane movie stars of the thirties and forties.

"You could embarrass a fellow, staring at him like that," he said softly, running his fingers through his thick dark wavy hair.

"Oh, nothing to be embarrassed about. I was just comparing you to William Powell and Cary Grant."

"You've got a case, you know that?"

"Mm-hmm," Maddy said complacently. She ate the last of her hash.

"How do you do that?" Clark asked.

She looked at him inquiringly.

"The way you always manage to make it work out so that you have a last bite of egg to go with the last bite of hash."

"Great sense of spatial relations, my old math professor used to tell me."

Instantly Maddy knew she'd said the wrong thing.

"Damn, oh, damn!" Clark swore softly, making a fist of his right hand and pounding the air. "You were so good in math, so good in everything at college." Shaking his head angrily, he said, "Sometimes I feel as though we'll never get back."

The newly wed Maddy and Clark had spent just a year studying at the University of Michigan when Clark's father, John, first showed symptoms of Alzheimer's Disease. Clark was an only child; his mother had been rendered frail by arthritis. Clark and Maddy gave up their plans for summer travel so they could take over the management of Whelan's Greenhouse.

When fall approached, Clark told Maddy he didn't see how he could go back to school. John Whelan had borrowed heavily to move and expand the greenhouse; then the economy had crunched. Clark felt he had to stay in Honeydale to help try to get the greenhouse back on solid footing. Though he had a football scholarship, and Maddy was also receiving financial aid from the university, there remained his parents' financial needs. John's doctors talked soberly about nursing homes; if this was his father's fate, Clark wanted the home to be the very best.

"I'll stay with you," Maddy had insisted, brooking no arguments. "It's only a semester."

Then Maddy had gotten pregnant. Though the pregnancy wasn't planned, neither she nor Clark felt anything but joy. The Whelans all needed an infusion of hope, and childbirth was the epitome of hope. Maddy willingly pushed back her plans to return to college. No point in starting while she was pregnant because she'd only drop out again. Even if Clark turned the greenhouse into a gold mine and they could afford the most expensive nurse, she wanted to be at home with her child for at least its first three years.

She looked into work she could do from home and got involved with the Mother Earth line. Selling suited her gregarious nature, and she believed that the products were honest. Her commissions kept mounting.

Meanwhile Clark transformed the greenhouse from a "bucket shop" into a place where beauty dwelled. Customers were encouraged to buy flowers by the stem instead of by the bunch. He hired a young florist from San Francisco who specialized in airy arrangements against the starkness of bare branches. Whelan's Greenhouse still handled Teleflorist orders and made up conventional arrangements for weddings and funerals, but their reputation for artistry was spreading.

Money remained very tight, however. Though all nuance seemed lost on John Whelan, Clark still insisted he have the finest care. Maddy encouraged him. The more the world around her seemed to become obsessed with mere things, the more willing she was to do without. There would be time for her and Clark to get an education and pick up the threads of old dreams. For John Whelan there wasn't much time.

He had died the year the girls started kindergarten. But the bills lingered on. Interest charges soared on old loans of John's that Clark was religiously struggling to pay off.

Maddy's parents would have given anything to help, but they had no resources. Retired school teachers, they lived simply in Arizona on a fixed income.

Now Clark looked at Maddy in the hard light of the Olympus Diner. "Don't worry," he said softly. "I won't lose faith. As long as you're with me, I'll keep hoping. Forgive the gloom of a moment, okay?"

Maddy's smile told him no forgiveness was needed. "Maybe I'll win the Wild Wind Granola Sweepstakes," she said lightly. "Or the Best-Buy Heavy-Duty Aluminum Foil jingle contest. What rhymes with 'heavy duty'?"

"You do." Clark kissed her fingertips. "You rhyme with everything. Lord, I love you. You really don't care if we're rich or not, do you? It never once crossed your mind that I should be more dedicated to your comfort, and the girls', rather than to my father's comfort and honor. Dilly!" Clark waved the waitress over. "Is there any champagne in the house? Maddy says it tickles her nose, but there are moments that demand champagne."

Dilly gave one of her snorts. "We've got Miller on tap. The champagne of beers. Bud and Heineken in bottles."

"Would you think me hopelessly unromantic if I had rice pudding instead?" Maddy looked at Clark through batting eyelids.

"You like it with raisins? Cook made it with raisins today," Dilly said.

"And the raisins are sun-dried champagne grapes, of course," Clark said. "Bring us two, please, Dilly. Heavy on the whipped cream. Spare no expense." He made private eyes at Maddy. "Champagne tonight," he vowed. "And other things."

"Heavy on the other things," she said, nudging his foot with hers. Instantly electric coils snaked through the air, binding her body to his. Let us go on like this forever, she silently prayed. Let this sweetness never end. Best of all possible husbands in the best of all possible worlds. Let me be worthy of my fortune. Clark, and the girls, and rice pudding with raisins, too.

Chapter 2

MADDY HAD A THEORY ABOUT CHILDREN. They always knew unconsciously when their parents wanted to make love and some imp of perversity compelled them to interfere.

Kendra and Nellie, age eight, were ordinarily angelic at bedtime. Teeth got scrubbed, toilet visited, water drunk, parents kissed, and the last page of the chapter read by eight-thirty, no muss, no fuss. Not this Thursday night, though. Here it was almost ten, and they were still bouncing off the ceiling.

"Mommy, my tummy hurts."

"Mommy, if I don't have another drink of water, I'll die."

"Daddy, just one more knock-knock joke, please? You tell the best knock-knock jokes in the whole world."

"Mommy, are you sure there's a God? Sukie Smith says there isn't, and she's the smartest kid in our class."

"Daddy, I'm going to be a football player just like you when I grow up because Mommy says girls can do anything."

Clark, whom Maddy considered the most patient of fathers, finally said wearily, "What the hell is going on here tonight?"

"You know," Maddy said. She raised her eyebrows suggestively.

He chuckled. "You think so? Were we giving off such sparks at dinner?"

"Well, you kissed the back of my neck when you cleared my plate for dessert."

"Is that a complaint, Mrs. Whelan?"

Maddy shook her head. "Thought it was sweeter than dessert, Mr. Whelan. What did you think my of my mapple cake?"

"Mapple?"

"Maple apple. Just thought of the name."

"Oh, such a clever Maddy. It was delicious," Clark said.

"Delicious enough to win the Spring Run Maple Syrup Bake-Off?"

He ran tender fingers through the ruffled layers of her hair. "Honest answer?"

"Of course." She couldn't hold back a tiny frown of disappointment. "Though I guess you just gave me your answer."

"It's not that it wasn't terrific," Clark said, "but I couldn't taste the maple syrup. I would have guessed brown sugar. They probably want something more mapley, don't you think?"

"They probably do." Maddy sighed. "First prize is five thousand dollars and a vacation for two for a week in Vermont. Winner's choice of season. And there are ten runner-up prizes of a thousand dollars each. I wonder if a maple custard pie would work. Maybe with a walnut crust."

Clark put a restraining hand on her wrist. "I don't think this is the moment to head for the kitchen. Do you hear what I hear?"

Maddy cocked an ear. "I don't hear a thing."

"Exactly, my heart. Blessed nothing. I do believe our whirligigs have finally worn themselves out." His strong, blunt fingers traced a feathery line down her throat. "I'll go check."

As he tiptoed upstairs Maddy sank back into the comforting old green embrace of the couch. Thank heaven Clark had volunteered to go upstairs because she couldn't have walked at the moment to save her life. Unbelievable that his fingers on her throat could turn her body into a quivering, boneless thing. Unbelievable, but exquisitely true.

Even her vision was affected by those seconds of contact. A haze seemed to have undulated into the room, wrapping everything in gauze. The old Boston rocker in which she'd nursed the twins had a golden shimmer to it. The glass-topped coffee table in front of the couch was a misty early morning pond of silver, and the well-worn green and gold Rya rug had become a dewy lawn. The flecked-wool armchair and ottoman, which to normal eyes had all the charm of a sat-out tweed suit, seemed grand and graceful in the haze, like a dowager viewed by candlelight.

How extraordinary that he could rearrange the universe for her after ten years together.

He came bouncing softly down the stairs, thumb and forefinger in a victorious circle. His hands were on her instantly, moving frenetically over her body with a pleasing lack of rhythm; he was too desirous to be artful, said those hungry hands. There seemed to be no part of her he didn't want, no part of her that didn't want him. Her nipples leaped to his touch, and so, somehow, did her collarbone.

"My dear woman," he said, with a little groan.

Maddy started; she shivered. "Oh, Clark, do you remember?"

"Remember what, love?" He traced bold paths down the inside of her blue-jeaned thigh; gasping, she obediently parted her legs.

"The first time we went out, and then we drove back to my house and you parked in my driveway. I don't think I was breathing at all. You came at me as delicately as if I were a butterfly. You kissed me and you said, 'My dear woman.' I didn't know until then that I'd stopped being a girl and really was a woman. Or maybe it was your kiss that ripened me. And those words."

"My best line. All the guys on the football team used it. Claimed they always scored."

"No!" Maddy protested, her legs clanging shut and trapping his hand.

"No," Clark conceded, tender laughter welling up, his lips apologizing to hers with dozens of tiny kisses. "The words just came out. Because you made me feel like a man, instead of the boy I'd been a couple of hours before. That stillness of yours, and your scent filling the air. Pure warm honey and a whiff of something wicked, too. That's still the way you smell and still the way I feel."

"You do feel exactly like a man," she said, her voice a mere thread but her hands aggressive. Her slender body thrilled as she found and captured the physical proof of her words.

He made a humming sound in her ear, and she thought of celestial fingers plucking at some miraculous silken harp. "Maddy. My love. My love." Then, earthy again, in time to keep her from swooning, he said, "Let's get you out of these damn clothes."

Maddy shrugged off her cotton knit sweater, jeans, and delicate thong sandals in a few fluid motions. She never wore a bra, and her perky breasts rose to meet the coolish air.

"Ah, my lawfully wedded breasts," Clark said, happily irreverent. "Sometimes I can't believe you really nursed two children." Wonderingly, he traced the tip-tilted profiles.

"I'm glad you still think they're nice." Maddy looked down, her fingers wandering where his had been.

"Nice as ever. No, don't take your hands away. I love to see you touch yourself. I want you to know what my hands feel. And you like it, don't you?"

"The sensation?" She gravely rubbed her nipples. "Or watching you watch me?"

"Both. Yes. Don't stop."

She cupped her hands over her breasts, and a moan escaped her lips.

"Beautiful. So beautiful," he said, encouraging her.

As if they had a life of their own, her hands slid down her belly, then stopped at the lacy edge of her sea-green bikini panties.

"Don't stop now."

Maddy looked at him, started to slide her panties over her hips, then laughingly shook her head. "You undress, too. I have to see that fabulous body."

"You want to see what you're doing to me."

"Oh, I know what I'm doing to you. I just need you to be naked with me."

Clark unbuttoned his shirt. "Not as spectacular a display as you offer."

"Are you kidding?" She thrust her hands into the soft tangle of hair on his chest. "Don't you know this is as beautiful a sight to me as I am to you? As if I were in some enchanted wood, cavorting with the king of beasts."

He roared softly, playing and yet not playing, and her blood began to dance. She caressed the muscles of his chest and shoulders, as firm and vibrant as they'd been in his quarterback days.

"Your body's more amazing in a way," she said, "because you made it what it is. Mine just happened."

Clark shook his head. "Your body is what it is because your mind is what it is. Your soul."

"There are wonderful human beings who have saggy breasts," Maddy said.

"I know, but I'm still right about you. You're all of a piece. And what a piece."

"He not only ogles, he leers." She basked in the sunshine of his praise. "Need a little help getting your pants off?"

"If you think I—"

"Mommy? Daddy?" A sleepy voice piped through the night. Maddy and Clark stopped cold.

Maddy heard the sounds of small feet scampering toward the master bedroom. A small fist rapped on the bedroom door, then turned the handle. "Mommy? Daddy?" The voice verged on a wail.

"Kendra, darling? We're down here," Maddy called out, hurriedly groping for clothing. In her haste she grabbed Clark's shirt, but never mind. The room was darkish; Kendra would be glazed with sleep. And Clark was decent enough in his khaki pants. "Did you have a bad dream?"

A solemn little redhead nodded, and a fey night-gowned body came running down the stairs and into Maddy's arms. "I dreamed I was getting on the school bus with Nellie, and she got on but I got left behind. So I ran to the next stop, but the bus got there first and went away without me. I saw Nellie in the window, and I knew she saw me, but she couldn't make the driver wait. It was so awful." The small body trembled.

Maddy cradled her, and Clark reached over to stroke the long silky strands of bright hair.

"It's all gone now," Maddy said. "Blown away with the wind. You know that could never happen, sweetie girl. Nellie would make the bus wait." Even as she said the words, she knew they weren't quite true. Nellie seemed to have been given an extra helping of talents when she was born. She was that little bit brighter in her school work, that little bit better at sports, that little bit more of a classic beauty. If Kendra was world-class, Nellie was state of the art. She might not always be able to wait for Kendra.

Kendra burrowed silently into her mother's warmth, and Maddy automatically began to rock her, strains of old lullabies coming back to mind and mouth from long ago.

Suddenly Kendra said, "You smell like Daddy."

"Do I?" Maddy said brightly, rocking faster, as if her daughter were still a baby who could be tricked into falling asleep. "I borrowed his shirt."

"You did?" How come?"

"Oh, just for fun. The way you and Nellie swap things sometimes."

"But we're the same size," Kendra said, relentlessly logical even in her half-awake state. "Grown-ups are weird."

"What do you say to a ride upstairs from your weird daddy? Or are you too sophisticated for me to carry you?" Clark asked.

"I'm not very sophisticated in the middle of the night," Kendra said accurately. "Come on, Daddy Taxi."

Clark scooped her up.

"Hey, your chest tickles. You should have put on Mommy's shirt."

"Ha-ha. Quiet now, or you'll wake up Nellie."

"'Night, Mom," Kendra called out in an exaggerated whisper.

"Good night, darling. Sweet dreams." Maddy gave a little wave of her hand, watching bemusedly as Daddy Taxi proceeded up the stairs, his meter ticking.

"One kiss. Two kisses. Three kisses. Four kisses. I hope you can pay for this ride, lady."

"Oh, yes," Kendra said, "and I'll give you a thousand hugs for your tip."

In five minutes, Maddy thought, Clark would come back and be ardent anew. And in the morning Kendra would be slick and worldly, turning the radio to the disco station, asking for shirred eggs because Sukie Smith had shirred eggs for breakfast, dropping words like "outrageous" and "splendid" into the table talk.

What was it Clark had said about her at lunch? That she was a marvelously contradictory woman. They all were, Maddy decided, sitting alone in the half light waiting for Clark to come back. All the Whelans; all the people on Earth. Saints and sinners, naïfs and sophisticates, fanatic strivers and playboys: Even the most extreme types were sometimes turned inside out. Thus the sense of possibility she awoke with every morning. The smallest acts of dailiness might turn into wild adventure because no one—and therefore nothing—was truly predictable.

She looked up and smiled as Clark came down the stairs.

"Now, where was I?" he said, diving for the couch, gathering her up.

"About to jump on my bones."

"I was, was I?"

"Unless," she said, "you're too full of Kendra's kisses."

"My, my. Competing with your own daughter." Clark's eyebrows arched up in genuine surprise.

"Heavens, no. Never. But a little girl's kisses are ultimate innocence. To make the switch to wickedness so quickly . . . Then again, I was just thinking how good we all are at sudden turnabouts." Maddy's fingers slalomed down his chest. "Want to go upstairs?"

Clark hesitated, and her heart sank. The spell was broken; people weren't infinitely capable of contradiction, after all.

But he was only saying, "I don't know. I was liking the feel of the couch. We could put down a towel . . ."

Maddy threw back her head and laughed. "That's what I get for conjuring up memories of high school."

"What's so bad?" He unbuttoned one of the buttons on her shirt. His shirt. Fingers sneaking in through the gap, he delicately stroked the satiny undersides of her breasts. "Bring back the old delicious guilt, the fear of getting caught."

"We *might* get caught. And it would hardly be delicious."

He shook his head. "Those girls are conked out until morning.

21

Noon, if we let them. It's going to be slogging through molasses to the school bus. Lord, I love your mouth," he said, shifting gears so suddenly that she caught her breath. "Those juicy lips . . ." He pulled her to him and covered her mouth with his. "Drink to me only with thy lips," he mumbled, nonsensical, passionate.

Her knees shook, and strange heat invaded her center as his lips pressed home, forcing her mouth open. His tongue was an invader—no, a liberator—and her heart danced a wild jig of welcome. Yet something in her resisted as though all armies, even friendly ones, had to be regarded with suspicion. "Yield," his tongue commanded. "You must give me yourself in order to have yourself." At last her tongue matched his for eagerness.

They were lying on the couch, and she didn't know how they'd gotten there: fallen, floated, been flung by the force of their need.

"Towel," she mumbled.

"We'll use my shirt," he said, pulling it off her and draping it under her.

He eased out of his khakis and ground his hips against hers.

"More," she demanded, loving his weight, wanting him to press her through the sat-out cushions into eternity. Then it was no longer enough to have him on her, and she begged him to be in her.

Putting one hand beneath the small of her back, he lifted her up to him and shared the burden of his heft. Her nipples grazed against his chest, her lips remained fused with his, and now came the ultimate joining.

A minute was all she needed to know paradise; yet an hour, a year, would not have been too much. A positive explosion of sweetness; sugar in the sky for an early Fourth of July.

"MW loves CW," she said on the wings of a sigh. The words that went without saying but always went better said.

"CW loves MW." Whispery kisses in her hair. "CW adores MW."

"CW and MW had better get their fannies up to their bedroom before they fall asleep," she said. "And put this incriminating shirt in the hamper."

"If we get found out, I'll marry you," he said.

"And if we don't get found out?"

"I'll marry you," he said.
"I have two kids," she said.
"I love kids," he said.
They went upstairs.

Chapter 3

CHAMPAGNE," CLARK SAID.

"Mmm?" Morning light was filtering in through the windows: a clear, perfect April day. Maddy wasn't quite ready for it. She buried her face against Clark's welcoming chest.

"I forgot the champagne last night. Being so intoxicated with you, and all."

"'S okay, darlin'," Maddy said, her words lazy. She yawned hugely. "Don't know why I'm so sleepy." Patting Clark's arm, she added, "You can get some 'nother time."

"But that's the thing. I got it. Sneaked it home in a plain brown paper bag and stuck it away in the refrigerator behind the apple juice."

"Oh, Clark, how sweet." She turned her back to him, burrowing in, inviting him to spoon his arms around her.

"Not sweet. *Brut.*"

"You're a sweet brute. Really, you are. We can have it for breakfast, if you like. Scrambled champagne. But the girls might report us."

"My daughters finks?" Clark nipped at the back of her neck. "Never. Go back to sleep, darling. You don't have to be up for another twenty minutes."

"Now he tells me."

Gently stroking the invisible line where her simple dotted-Swiss white nightgown made a shallow scalloped wave across her breasts, he said, "I'll sing you a lullaby. All about how beautiful you are." His hands caressed her rhythmically as he crooned, "Beautiful, beautiful, beautiful Maddy, makes me glad and never saddy. Beautiful, beautiful, beautiful Maddy—"

Maddy sat bolt upright, scattering his hands, the sheets, the patchwork quilt Clark's mother had made for them. "Beautifoil!" she exclaimed.

"Hello?" Clark said gently, as though fearing she'd flipped.

"The jingle! I've got it! And you did it for me. Listen." Eyes aluminum-bright, she recited, "Best-Buy Heavy-Duty Foil makes my life more beautifoil."

"Beautifoil," Clark echoed, tasting the word. "I like it, honey."

"A lot?"

"A lot." He nodded vigorously. "It's really got pizzazz. Beautifoil. It's simple, and sort of funny, and it's . . . I don't know . . . different. As though maybe there's more to foil than catching greasy drippings in the oven."

"Exactly." Maddy clapped her hands with the innocent egoism of a child. "And there *is* more to foil than that. When I want to steam my skin, I make a tent of foil over the bathroom sink, run the water at its hottest, and it's an instant facial sauna."

Clark ran his fingertips over the silk of her cheeks. "So that's your secret, you vixen. Too bad you can't tell the contest judges."

"But I can! There's a bonus offered if the winning entry is accompanied by a photograph showing an original use of Best-Buy Heavy-Duty Aluminum Foil."

Hugging her, Clark said, "You do have a wonderful toy shop of a mind. Do we have film for the Polaroid? I'll take a shot before I leave for the greenhouse."

"We're all out," Maddy said lightly, not mentioning that she'd balked at that particular expense for the past few weeks. "Anyway, the entrant has to take the photograph. Fortunately. I don't want you seeing me with my face all covered with sweaty oatmeal."

"Oatmeal. Of course."

"It's terrific for taking out the impurities."

Clark pushed back her hair and flicked her ear with his tongue. "You have no impurities."

"Oh, I do," she said, her face suddenly grave. "I love you impurely. As well as purely. That's the way it's supposed to be, isn't it?" She stared into the gleaming gray of his eyes.

"Maybe so," he said huskily. "I just know that we're the way it's supposed to be." Unable to suppress a groan, he said, "I want you."

Maddy lay back on her pillow, pulling the delicious roughness of his unshaven face down to her breasts. "You have me. Forever. Which is a good thing because the alarm is about to go off."

The small digital clock on her side of the bed went "ping, ping, ping."

"On top of everything else, she's psychic," Clark declared, his strong arms going around her, his nose making an admiring foray into her raspberry-scented hair. "Or just damn smart. I remember reading that the ability to intuit the time is a function of IQ. What a woman!"

"I hate to disillusion you, lover, but I was looking at the clock." With a little laugh, and a flurry of kisses for his forehead, she sat up. "Who's going to have the joy of awakening the girls this morning?"

"I think it's going to require a team effort." Giving Maddy a last covetous look, he swung his long legs out of bed, reached for the red-and-white-striped robe hanging on the bedpost, and stood up.

Waking the girls turned out to be a snap; they were as serene and cooperative as they'd been impossible the night before. Maddy made a mental note to remember this morning the next time the girls slept eleven hours and woke up cranky and slow.

The whole day seemed charmed, in fact. Two Mother Earth customers called up and placed big orders for vitamins and cosmetics. The mail brought a money order from a third customer who'd given Maddy two bad checks. Sympathetic with anyone strapped for cash—though she had never bounced a check in her life—Maddy had covered the checks herself rather than hound the woman. To her happy surprise, the money order was accompanied by a heartfelt note thanking her for her kindness.

A charmed day. Definitely. The air was warm and sweet, washed clean by the downpour of the day before. The forsythia bushes were bursts of yellow, bright as scrapings from the surface of the sun, deflecting the eye from the weathered paint on the front of the house and one listing shutter that refused to stay fixed. Spring was absolute now, not just a promise; snow would not fall again that season. Maddy flexed her arms, left bare by a short-sleeved blue cotton knit sweater worn with cropped blue-and-yellow-striped pants, and exulted in her freedom.

The charm held. The camera store was having a special on Polaroid film. The supermarket yielded up early strawberries, astonishing Maddy's nose with their perfume. A cantaloupe promised to be ready in a day or two.

Nicest of all, Jill Laverty announced that she wasn't going to enter the Best-Buy jingle contest. Jill and Con Laverty were probably the Whelans' closest friends. For all her love of competition, Maddy had no taste for going up against someone she cared about. The thrill lay in pitting herself against anonymous thousands of minds. Jill shared Maddy's love of games, but she preferred sweepstakes, which were strictly a matter of luck, to contests involving skills.

Anyway, she told Maddy over the telephone, she'd used up her monthly postage allowance by entering the Wild Wind Granola Sweepstakes fifty separate times. For dedicated contesters, postage was no small matter. The Internal Revenue Service allowed the cost of stamps to be deducted only if one had winnings to declare. So far the biggest win either woman had scored was an "oral prophylaxis"— otherwise known as a tooth cleaning—which Jill had won in a drawing at the Honeydale Junior High winter bazaar. Since Con was a dentist, Jill had been less than thrilled.

"Well, I'm entering the Best-Buy contest," Maddy told her friend.

"Aha! Got a good one?"

"I think so. 'Best-Buy Heavy-Duty Foil makes my life more beauti-foil.'" Maddy waited anxiously for her friend's response. Jill wasn't one for mincing words.

"Oh, Maddy! I love it!" There was no denying the sincerity in Jill's voice. "And—wait—I'll bet you're sending a snapshot of that thing you do with the sink, right?"

"Right," Maddy said happily.

"Honey, I think this is it. The big one. Those Best-Buy people are very image-conscious, you know. Low prices and all that, but the packaging is very snazzy, not like those black-and-white generic horrors that make me feel embarrassed at the check-out."

"Since you like it, will you come pose in my steamy sink picture?"

"You're the one who should be in it," Jill said. "Those smoldering eyes."

"Never mind smoldering. You're the one with the all-American face. Say you will. You'll bring me luck."

"They're not offering oral prophylaxis as tenth prize, are they?"

Half an hour later, Jill—complete with button nose, freckles, and a grin made more endearing by a gap between her front teeth—drove into the Whelans' driveway. "Hope you're going to fix the potholes with your prize money," she grumbled good-naturedly. "Though, gee, with five hundred grand you'll probably get a new house. You'll be up in Hondeydale Hills, I suppose. And the girls will go to Honeydale Prep . . ."

Putting an affectionate hand on her friend's arm, Maddy said, "These days five hundred thousand dollars buys you either a new house *or* private school for two. Anyway," she added, "I had an attack of insecurity while you were on the way over here. I'm not going to win first prize. I'll be lucky if I win a *Best-Buy Cookbook*."

"Maddy Whelan, you, who've given me a thousand lectures on the value of positive thinking? You're going to win, all right. Can I take another look at the prize list? I threw away my entry blank last week so I wouldn't be tempted."

Looking at the list, Maddy couldn't help laughing. Contests and sweeps were a cosmic joke. Such ridiculously grandiose prizes that they had no connection with ordinary reality. What would she do with five hundred thousand dollars? And a trip to Venice for two? And— as a bonus if she submitted a photo—a wardrobe by "the sensational young designer" Donatello?

I'd give it all away, one voice in her head suggested. But she knew she wouldn't. She was a nice person, not ungenerous, but she didn't have pretensions to sainthood, and she rather resented people who did. She'd give some of it away, and the rest she'd enjoy to pieces with Clark and the girls. Then she'd get back to her everyday life in the house where they'd all been so happy. Filled potholes, yes; Honeydale Hills, no.

"Who's this Donatello?" Jill asked. "I thought he was a sculptor." Unabashedly clothes-mad, she spent most of her substitute teacher's pay on her wardrobe and knew all the big designers' names.

"Yes, about five hundred years ago," Maddy said. "I've never heard of the designer. Or have I? Wait a minute," she said suddenly, clapping her hand over her mouth. She ran upstairs and came back down brandishing the red and silver scarf she'd worn to lunch with Clark the day before. "Look," she chortled, pointing to a scrawled signature woven into the design.

"I don't believe it!" Jill exclaimed. "It's a sign, kiddo. I can see it now," she went on, sighing. "Designer meets contest winner. Designer is stunned by contest winner's leggy body. Designer asks contest winner to model for him." She gestured at her own neat but unremarkable figure. "If I won, he'd ask me to take cash instead of his clothes."

Maddy playfully swatted her friend. "Come on. Let's go upstairs and take that photograph and get you discovered as a model.

"Beautifoil, beautifoil," she hummed, as she set about transforming the upstairs bathroom into a spa. Really, it didn't take all that much transforming. It was a small room, but pretty, with flowered tiles set at random among the solid pink tiles. The vanity had a graceful oval basin, and set over it was an old-fashioned hand-painted wooden medicine chest, the sort she'd been told was all the rage now. The vanity had a pot of fresh pink flowers on it—a snapdragon, a tulip, a sweetheart rose, and a perfect Gerber daisy with its outsize head. Flowers were one traditional luxury item that came free to the Whelan household. Clark always brought home what he called the "widows and orphans," flowers with broken stems or ragged leaves or some other imperfection that rendered them unsalable. Maddy took special pleasure in giving these blooms a few extra days of life.

Maddy moved the family's toothbrushes out of camera range, then moved them back again. Her snapshot was supposed to show

how aluminum foil could transform an ordinary bathroom into something . . . beautifoil.

She pulled a good yard of foil off the roll she'd brought up with her and tented it over the basin, wrapping the ends of the foil under the edges of the vanity. Using another yard of foil, she encompassed the faucet as well. She placed the Best-Buy box on the side of the vanity, slightly weighting the foil and very definitely showing off the manufacturer's logo. She turned on the hot water.

"Wow!" Jill said reverently, as steam began accumulating under the foil tent. "It really works."

"I told you," Maddy said with a laugh. She took a pink towel and wound it into a turban around Jill's head. Opening a jar with a Mother Earth label on it, she stroked cream onto her friend's face.

"Ugh! Oatmeal." Jill wrinkled her nose.

"It's a lovely smell," Maddy protested. "And terrific for your skin."

Jill folded her arms across her ample chest. "This whole 'beautifoil' business was a trap. All these years of resisting Mother Earth, and now I'm covered in it."

"Shh! Never you mind. Stick your head under the tent, as the witch said to Gretel. Deep breaths. It's great for the sinuses." Backing across the room and standing against the tub, Maddy focused the camera.

"It's hot," Jill complained.

"I hope so." Maddy snapped the shutter. "Now, I want to try one with your face showing. Are you sweating yet?"

"I'll say."

"Okay, turn around and face me. Gorgeous!"

After six more shots Maddy declared that Jill could be released from her purgatory. She gently stroked off the oatmeal cream with cotton saturated in an orange-scented astringent. Using a special mister, she treated Jill's face to a cool taste of mineral water; then she turned Jill around and directed her toward the mirror. "What do you think?"

A foolish look of pleasure crept across Jill's face. "Wow! Kind of pink, but wow!"

"The pink will go away in an hour. The 'wow!' will stay for days. Now, if I can just find my order pad," she teased.

"Don't you dare hustle me, Maddy Whelan, you, who are about

to be fabulously rich. But maybe just a small jar of the unspeakable oatmeal goop . . ."

Maddy laughed. "Not until you see how you like your skin in a couple of days. Anyway, if you start buying Mother Earth, it'll sully our friendship. Let's go downstairs and have some mint tea and mapple cake."

"Mapple?" Jill said. "Don't tell me. Maple apple for the Spring Run Bake-off."

"Yes, except that I'm not entering the cake. Clark says it isn't mapley enough."

"You don't need a lousy five grand," Jill said as they started down the stairs, her voice suddenly sober. "And I don't need mapple cake, not if I'm going to skinnify myself enough to wear your used Donatellos. Got your lucky pen? I want you to fill in the entry form while I watch. You don't want to blow it."

Maddy nodded knowingly. The smallest mistake—a ZIP code left out, or typing used where hand-printing was specified in the rules—could get an entry disqualified. Sitting at the kitchen table after Jill had left, she hand-printed her jingle on scratch paper half a dozen times. Then she took a deep breath and carefully copied it onto the official entry from, using a fine-point turquoise felt-tip pen she'd found—just found—in her purse one day.

She fanned out the Polaroid pictures, frowning with concentration. She thought of waiting until Clark came home, or asking Jill's opinion, but she really didn't have the right to put that burden on someone else's shoulders. If she lost, she didn't want Clark or Jill feeling responsible. And really, she told herself, she was going to lose. "Beautifoil" was cute, but it wasn't incandescent. Her photographs were definitely amateurish. With a mental shrug of her shoulders she picked the second shot she'd taken—Jill grinning cutely and the words "Best-Buy" prominent. She quickly addressed and stamped the envelope, adorning it with hearts and flowers and other good-luck, eye-catching flourishes beloved by contest folk. There. Done. Over and out. Up to the fates.

Chapter 4

S HE WON.

The letter came on a day in May so crazy that she didn't open the mail until two, just let it lie in its basket underneath the mail slot. Crazy: Nellie home from school with a belly ache and a fever of one hundred one—and the class play (in which she was starring) was set for the following evening! Crazy: Mother Earth had bungled Maddy's last order and sent two cases of brewer's yeast, for which she had no customers, and none of the aloe tanning lotion and new Natural Slimming Tea, for which she had dozens of orders. Crazy: Clark calling with the news that there had been an accident; his delivery man had run a red light. No one had been seriously hurt, but the van was badly dented, and the Cunningham wedding flowers were all but totaled.

The letter came in an ordinary-looking number-ten white envelope, identified only by a cryptic return address, a post office box in Chicago. Maddy bothered to read a postcard from Montreal first, from a former neighbor and Mother Earth client who had moved three months ago.

Her mind was full of Clark and Nellie; she was tensing up for the next telephone call, the next moan from upstairs, as she opened the envelope. Then she saw the logo of the J. J. Harrington Company, well-known contest judges, and her heart began to hammer. All thoughts fell away.

She'd won! "Beautifoil" had done it. "Dear Ms. Whelan, Heartiest Congratulations." Grand prize plus the bonus. Conditional only on her signing the enclosed affidavit and release form.

Her throat went so dry she thought she was going to choke. Letting the letter dangle from her fingers as though serious contact might burn her, she floated to the kitchen and guzzled water. She sat down at the kitchen table and read the letter again. Held it upside down, shook it, and read it once more. There was no mistaking the words. She'd won.

She added ice to her water and began to dial the number of Whelan's Greenhouse. Then she clicked the disconnect button. A joke, a hoax, a mistake. It had to be. She couldn't—giggles starting now—she couldn't really have won.

Heartiest congratulations. Five hundred thousand dollars. A trip to Venice for two. A wardrobe by Donatello.

Dear Lord, did You do me this kindness? Let me be worthy of Your gift.

Clark! she shouted in her head. We're free! No more debts! No potholes! I won!

She refilled her water glass. She dialed the telephone number printed on the Harrington letterhead. No need to wait until evening rates were in effect; she could call anywhere anytime now. Oh, Nellie and Kendra, do you believe this? Jill, I won!

"J. J. Harrington," a female voice said, its twang excitingly Midwestern to Maddy's ear.

The buzz in Maddy's mind subsided. "Contest judging department, please," she said, as if she were any old person calling.

"I'm sorry, we don't give out information about contests over the telephone," Chicago recited. "If you want the list of winners for a contest, kindly send a self-addressed, stamped envelope with the name of the contest in the lower left-hand corner."

"I just received a letter telling me that I'm a winner." Maddy squashed the giggle that threatened to rise in her again. "I'd like confirmation, please."

"I'll transfer you to Mr. Bullock," Chicago said abruptly.

As the wires hummed, Maddy considered hanging up. It was a cruel, awful, terrible joke, but wonderful for a moment; she wouldn't really be mad at whomever had played it.

"Bullock," said a crunchy New York voice.

"This is Madeline Whelan, in Honeydale, New York. I just received—"

"Beautifoil Madeline Whelan! Congratulations, Mrs. Whelan!"

"Oh, heaven." The words came out in a mouse squeak. "It's true? I won?"

"Assuming neither you nor anyone in your immediate family is an employee of The Best-Buy Corporation; the McIntee, Swift, and Wumper Advertising Agency; or the J. J. Harrington Company."

"No," she said faintly.

The man at the other end of the telephone chuckled. "You sound worried, Mrs. Whelan. Don't be worried. Enjoy. Winning is what you always wanted, isn't it?"

His words echoed in her head as she hung up and went to fish the affidavit of eligibility and consent form out of the envelope. The "affy," as contesters called it, was easy; she didn't even know anyone who knew somebody who worked for Best-Buy, their ad agency, or Harrington.

The consent form was another matter. If she signed it, she gave Best-Buy the right not only to her beautifoil jingle, but also to the use of her name and "likeness" in advertising and promotion. With a little shiver, she remembered that anyone who sent the J. J. Harrington Company a self-addressed, stamped envelope could receive a list with her name on it.

"Mama." Nellie's pain-laden voice floated down from upstairs. Her shiver turning into a chill, Maddy realized that all thought of her ailing child had fled from her mind since she'd opened the momentous letter. Was this what winning did to a soul? Preserve us all, she begged.

She took the stairs two at a time. One look into the twins' red and white menagerie—the shelter for wounded stuffed animals, Clark had dubbed it—and relief took the edge off her guilt. The flush had subsided from Nellie's pearlescent skin. Her gray eyes shone with mischief again.

"Mama, I'm desperate for ginger ale." The voice of pain was pure drama, thank the Lord—enough to sustain the entire third-grade play.

"You're feeling better, aren't you, sweetie?" Maddy's hand on Nellie's forehead confirmed what her eyes had seen. Nellie's temperature was normal.

"Not all the way better." With her oval face, and black hair hanging to her shoulders, Nellie could look like Elizabeth Barrett Browning in her waning days if she wanted to, especially when she was wearing an old-fashioned high-necked white nightgown. "I'd say it's still touch and go. But ginger ale would save me."

"Well, we'd better save you, hadn't we?" Maddy plumped up two pillows clothed in mismatched cases. In a flash she mentally redid the room: a delicate flowered wallpaper covering the grubby red and white stripes; swag curtains on the two windows; lovely old quilts and embroidered sheets on the beds. And why not the bunk beds the girls had clamored for—so much fun for slumber parties—instead of their standard-issue twin beds?

Pleasure and dismay fought to possess her mind. The room would be beautiful, but swag curtains? She and Clark had made their girls realize early on that *things* were not the key to happiness. The room was beautiful as it was, reflecting the girls' affectionate natures. At the rate she was going, she'd soon have a scheme for replacing Kendra's and Nellie's heart-tugging collection of eyeless, lop-eared, balding stuffed animals with pristine creatures from FAO Schwarz.

"Are you okay, Mom?" Nellie was looking at her with real concern, the phony pain gone from her voice.

"I'm fine, sweetie." Maddy hesitated, wondering whether to tell Nellie her news. But it wasn't fair for Nellie to hear before Kendra did, and really not right for the girls to hear before Clark did. "Let me get you your ginger ale. Meanwhile, go wash your hands and face and give your hair a brushing."

"You always say that when we're sick." Nellie looked longingly at the mystery lying face down on her blanketed knees. "It's more important for me to read, isn't it?"

"Reading is one of the most important things in the world. But your book won't go away." Maddy held out her hand. "Come on, Nell. Your face looks like something Nancy Drew could find a dozen clues in. Yuk!"

Nellie giggled. Scampering out of bed, she took her mother's hand. Maddy's heart gave a squeeze of joy. Without notice, the joy changed to fear. Five hundred thousand dollars. Her name in the papers. The girls would be targets for kidnappers, like the rich kids in Honeydale Hills. Relief swept over her as she remembered: The Internal Revenue Service would probably take half her winnings. Once again the desire to giggle rose up in her. Imagine being glad about being taxed!

Maddy delivered Nellie's ginger ale, then poured herself an iced mint tea and sat down to call Clark. But no, she thought, as she started to dial, this wasn't right at all. Not the telephone for news so big. She flashed back to the beautiful moment when she'd learned she was pregnant. Instead of calling Clark, or even telling him with words when he came home, she'd borrowed a scene from a classic Irish play. She'd set an extra place at the dinner table. When Clark had asked who was coming to dinner, she'd pointed to her belly. The day they'd heard two fetal heartbeats in the obstetrician's office, Clark had said, "You should have set a fourth plate."

Suddenly inspired, she ran to the old captain's trunk in the den where the grown-up games were kept, and she took out Monopoly. It was a game she had mixed feelings about. It was deliciously competitive, but it placed such emphasis on acquisition. Today, though, it would definitely suit her purpose. Taking out the brightly colored money, she realized it didn't total nearly five hundred thousand. Never mind. It would convey the idea.

Then to the bookshelves, to the special shelf where she and Clark lovingly preserved their books from college, still arranged according to subject. From the art history section, she took down John Ruskin's *Stones of Venice*. Thumbing through the book, she felt exquisite tremors travel up and down her spine as she looked at color plates of St. Mark's, the Doge's Palace, and the Contarini Fasan Palace on the Grand Canal. That one glorious year she and Clark had spent at the

University of Michigan, they'd taken a history-of-architecture course together. Holding hands, and more, when the lecturer dimmed the lights to show slides, they'd imagined themselves in every grand setting they saw.

Now the dream was alive again. She and Clark worshiping in St. Mark's . . . taking a gondola ride down the Grand Canal on a moonlit night . . . standing awed in front of the canvases of Titian and Tintoretto.

Monopoly money and *The Stones of Venice* in hand, Maddy went upstairs to her bedroom and opened her top bureau drawer. She took out the red and silver scarf designed by Donatello. This one time she folded it to show the designer's name.

She put everything in a silver gift box she'd saved from Christmas; she tied a red ribbon around it. Her heart was beating a foolish tattoo. She was thankful that Kendra would be home any minute, needing banal milk and cookies.

Then Clark was actually there, his footsteps light and his voice cheery despite the accident that day. "Where are my women?" he was calling out, as always, hungry for hugs and kisses.

Nellie was well enough to be dressed and downstairs; she and Kendra went for his knees. Maddy took the upper level.

Trembling with suppressed excitement and more than a little fear, she buried her face in his neck to keep from divulging all.

"What's up?" he asked her ear, punctuating his words with kisses. His fingers in her hair hinted at pleasures to come when the girls were asleep. "Titian," he said suddenly.

She reeled. "What?"

"I just found Titian red in your hair. Right here." He feathered a spot near her crown.

If she had needed a sign, here it was. But she was still doing battle with herself. "You found Titian years ago. Back in college." She could say "college" unemotionally because college loomed again.

"That was over here." His fingers traveled two or three inches. "This is a new Titian."

"Oh, yes," she said joyfully.

"Daddy," Kendra and Nellie said impatiently, wanting his attention.

He picked them up in one swift motion, as if they were still a pair of nurslings. Twirling them until they were all three breathless and chortling, he gently set them down. "All right, my Clarklings. I think your mama needs a word with me. You scoot out to the porch and do some reading until dinner. You finish that Nancy Drew, Nellie?"

The dark little head nodded. "And started another."

"We'll read some poems together later," Clark said. "Nancy Drew is fun, but enough's enough. What are you reading, Kendra?"

"Fairy tales. Baby stuff," she answered unabashedly.

"Not baby stuff at all. Fairy tales are for children of all ages. You know that expression?"

"Because everyone needs imagination," the red-haired child said. "Right, Daddy?"

"Right, hon. Imagination and big dreams and fairy tales help us to know the difference between good and bad."

"So does Nancy Drew," said Nellie, reminding Maddy of her own competitive nature. "Because there are good guys and bad guys."

Clark tousled her hair. "Yes. True. Now, let Mama and me have a little privacy."

As the girls ran off to the porch, Maddy shook her head with delight. If there had ever been a more loving and conscientious father than Clark, she couldn't imagine who, or how. With a few words he had managed to give Kendra's ego the infusion it needed and Nellie's the slight deflating it required. Leaning against him, she murmured words of praise.

"But that's not what you've been dying to tell me ever since I walked in the door," he said.

"No," she agreed. "No, you frighteningly prescient person. Come." She led him into the den. Waiting on an end table heaped with books due at the library was the red-ribboned silver box.

"For me?"

"For us. All of us. Oh, Clark." She bit her lips. Her fists were tight little balls.

His gray eyes full of questions, a smile tugging at the corners of his mouth, he picked up the box. He put it to his ear and shook it. He put it to his nose and sniffed it.

"Don't tease me," Maddy pleaded. "Open it. I can't wait another minute."

He opened it. He looked. "Monopoly money. Venice. A scarf," he recited. Suddenly his face all but exploded with delight. "Beautifoil? Oh, honey! Beautifoil?"

Maddy nodded mutely.

"Grand prize! The whole thing? Five hundred thousand dollars? Venice? The clothes by what's-his-name?"

Maddy pointed to the signature on the scarf. "That's his name. Donatello."

"Of course. Donatello. How could I have forgotten?" Donatello's sculpture of Mary Magdalene was a work of art they'd long ago vowed to go see in Florence. "Maddy? The whole thing?"

"The works," she said faintly.

With a great whoop, Clark swept her up into his arms. "Maddy, you astounding woman! Darling, I'm so proud of you!" His lips pressed hers in an ecstatic kiss. "Beautifoil, beautifoil Maddy!"

"It's all right?" she asked, looking up at him.

"All right?" he echoed, astonished. "You're not worried, are you? Maddy, you deserve to win. You deserve everything. Not just for being clever, but for being all the splendors you are." He eased her down onto the plaid convertible couch with weary springs that served as sitting place and sometime guest bed. "This calls for a celebration. I don't suppose you went out and bought champagne?"

She shook her head. "I was home with a sick kid, remember?"

"You could have had it delivered. You could have had a case delivered."

She looked at him, shocked. Champagne by the case . . . deliveries . . . How could she help but be corrupted? "We have some jug wine in the fridge," she said. "It was good enough for us last night."

"Maddy, Maddy." He sat down next to her and cradled her in his arms. "I've never seen you like this. I think you're in a state of shock. Feeling guilt, unworthiness, heaven only knows what." His strong fingers tilting her chin up toward him, he let his lips wander lightly over hers. "Darling, if I had won and weren't being ecstatic about it, you'd tell me I was being ungrateful."

He was right, and she knew it, but his words only made her feel shame on top of her other dire emotions. She remembered reading about a New York State Lottery winner who hadn't turned in her winning ticket for days because she was so confused. Maddy had felt little sympathy for the woman. If being a sore loser was wrong, being a sore winner was worse.

The Whelans were free now. She had won them freedom from debt, freedom from thinking about money. They would get their degrees and win the world. It didn't matter a hoot if they drank champagne or not, had it delivered or not. Poverty and wealth weren't virtues or vices in themselves; it was how you handled them that mattered. She and Clark had done a bang-up job of handling the absence of money; they would handle its presence with equal grace.

As long as she and Clark had each other, they could handle anything.

"Come on," she said, her old merry self, tugging at his hand. "Let's go spring the news on the girls."

Chapter 5

T HE LETTER ARRIVED ON WEDNESDAY. By Thursday the news was all over Honeydale.

Jill Laverty, sparkling with excitement for her friend, came by to help handle the telephone calls. Quickly spotting a pattern, she made a chart on her yellow legal pad. There were well-wishers—real; well-wishers—phony. Charities—real; charities—phony. One call came from an astrologer who knew, just knew, that Maddy was an Aquarius . . . a Scorpio? . . . a Gemini? Yes, she'd known all along that Maddy was a Libra. One woman claimed that "Beautifoil" was her idea and that Maddy had stolen it from her brain with the help of the CIA.

Maddy escaped from the jangling telephone into the world of ordinary errands, only to find that the news had preceded her there. The lines she heard were so wondrously absurd that she began writing them down each time she got back to the car.

Manager of the Econo-Shop Supermarket: "I suppose this is the last time you'll be asking me to okay a check, Mrs. Whelan. By next week you'll be sending the maid to Honeydale Hills Fine Imported Foods."

Clem of Clem's Cwik Cleaners (as he handed over a bunch of cleaning-by-the-pound-it's-cheaper-all-around): "I don't guess I'll be seeing these rags anymore."

Dana Smith (mother of Sukie, the twins' classmate): "You still out here delivering that Mother Earth goop? To tell you the truth, Maddy, I've only been buying because I admire the way you've been helping Clark undo the mess his father made."

John at the Honeydale Center Service Station: "Looks like you can get rid of the deathmobile now, Mrs. W. Have I got a Porsche for you!"

Maddy sought refuge in the Olde Tea Shoppe, a dark-paneled bastion of gentility; the elderly sisters who ran it either hadn't heard the news or were too discreet to bring it up. But when she was halfway through a dainty chopped-egg sandwich on airy white bread, her letter carrier dropped in for coffee. Setting his canvas sack down with a thud, he hurried over to her table. His words of congratulations quickly degenerated into a broad hint that she should reward "the messenger of glad tidings."

On Sunday morning even her minister, the gentle Dr. Goodale, seemed to be part of a conspiracy to discomfit her. He delivered a ringing sermon on receiving manna from heaven, followed none too subtly by a reference to the church's restoration fund.

Maddy declined, politely, to see a reporter from *The Banner*, a tabloid specializing in stories about drugs, sex, rock stars' divorces, miracle diets, and farmers' wives who gave birth to Martians. Five days later a story appeared:

> Madeline Whelan, who used to be what a neighbor called "the friendliest person in town," now shuts the door in people's faces. Winning five hundred thousand dollars does that sort of thing. Barricading herself in the white Colonial mansion she shares with her husband and twin daughters in exclusive Honeydale, New York . . .

Maddy wanted to laugh the story off, but she couldn't. She was still fretting as she and Clark got ready for bed.

"I deserve it," she decided, looking disconsolately in the mirror set over her chest of drawers. "I should have treated that reporter like a human being and invited her in."

"Don't be silly, Maddy," Clark said sharply. "If you'd done that, she would have written that you're a publicity hound. With some people you can't win."

She gave him a searching look. Those were unlikely words coming from her generous-spirited Clark. Stretched out on the bed in nothing but a pair of pale blue boxer shorts, he had an equally unlikely look on his face. Sullen. Dour. Angry.

"You're mad at me," she said wonderingly.

"No, I'm not. I'm just tired, frankly." He reached over and picked up a magazine that had fallen to the floor.

The dismissive gesture infuriated Maddy. "Oh, you're finally being frank with me," she said sarcastically. She took a brush to her hair with swift, hard strokes. "I think what you mean is, you're tired of anything to do with the contest."

"I admit I could do without being called 'Mr. Beautifoil.'" He opened the magazine.

Maddy crossed to the bed in two swift strides, grabbed the magazine from Clark's hands, and flung it to the floor. Then, aghast at what she had done, she burst into tears.

Clark sat up and folded her into his arms. "It's all right, darling. Never mind. It was my fault."

"It's not all right," she said between sobs. "We've been fighting all week long."

"I know. It's a strange time. We didn't foresee the rough stuff."

"I wish I'd never entered the contest." She licked a salty little puddle from his shoulder.

"Don't say that, Maddy. Look at all the good that's going to come of it. The house for my mother, for one thing. She says she feels twenty years younger already, just from thinking about living without stairs. Dick Grable at the bank wants to throw us a paper-burning party. And you should feel so proud of the girls' reactions. All they can think about is giving things to others, not getting."

Maddy tried to take comfort from his words, from the dear, familiar strength of his arms. But she just kept finding fresh worries. The girls were going to sleep-away camp in July, so she and Clark could go to Venice. They would have each other, and Clark's mother—their beloved Grandanna—would also be on call. But what if, God forbid, one of them got ill or fell off a horse? Their parents would be an ocean away. To make her guilt much worse, a part of her was ecstatic at the thought of having a second honeymoon with Clark.

But what kind of honeymoon would it be if she and Clark went on snapping at each other? How proud she'd been of their spirit these past ten years. Maybe she'd been too proud. It was one thing to be happy in the face of adversity, but another to be happy *because* of it.

What kind of honeymoon would it be if they didn't much make love? Since she'd learned about winning the contest, bed had been mostly for making war and for sleeping thick, dull sleeps.

"Listen," Clark said suddenly.

She listened. The sound of crickets chirping filled the night. Clark went to the windows and drew back the curtains. A moon just off the full bathed the room in a silver light.

A lazy June breeze played over Maddy's body, which was barely covered by a wispy turquoise shortie nightgown.

An air conditioner for their bedroom was on The List, and The List was affordable now, A to Z. Come August they would sleep in perfect comfort. Without cricket song, silver light, or sensual breeze.

I'll make a tape recording of crickets, she thought absurdly. "Make love to me, Clark," she said urgently, wanting him, wanting not to think.

"Anything else would be an insult to the moonlight." He lay down next to her, facing her, not quite touching her. Raising one hand, he traced a path in the air an inch above her. "Feel me?" He brought his hand back to her shoulder height and made the same motion again, still not touching her.

Suddenly she did feel him—felt something, anyway. A wild wave of heat that made her fine hairs stand on end. She closed her eyes, retreating to a secret room hung in red silk and velvet. "Where am I?" she whispered. "Do you know?"

"I think so. Don't open your eyes. It's the right place to be."

She heard him rearrange his body. Then she felt his breath snaking along her the way his hand had done, touching her without touching her, burning her without hurting her, taking her deeper into the room.

She felt his eyelashes then, making contact: what as children she and her friends had called butterfly kisses. Except that the butterfly kisses of her childhood had been innocent wings on cheeks. Clark's butterflies were as brazen as they were delicate, dancing underneath her nightgown across the hillocks of her breasts.

Her belly contracted as the butterflies danced their way south. "Clark," she said with a little gasp. "Dearest." Opening her eyes, she urged his head back up toward the pillow. "Kiss me. I'm starved for you."

"So demanding." He put a chiding finger to her cheek.

"Kiss me, _please_." She parted her lips invitingly.

He kissed her lower lip, her upper lip; he opened his mouth to cover hers. His hands eased off her nightgown and his shorts in one swift move.

The telephone rang.

"What the hell?" Clark exploded. It was nearly midnight. He grabbed the receiver. "Yes?" He listened for a moment, then wordlessly passed the instrument to Maddy.

"Hello?" she said dazedly, her senses still jangling.

"Madeline Whelan? This is Rip Mangione's Nightline on WMMM in Miami. You're on the air. And I'll bet you're up in the air. How does it feel to have won half a million dollars?"

"It feels grand," Maddy said automatically. Absurdly, she felt herself smiling, then blushing. Naked to all Miami! She wriggled under the sheet, pulling it up to her breast. She looked at Clark to share the joke, but he didn't laugh.

Rip Mangione was laughing, though. "I'll bet it _feels_ grand," he said expansively, as though Maddy's words had been infinitely wise and witty. "Five _hundred_ grand. What are you going to do with your winnings, Madeline Whelan?" The pitch of his voice changing, he went on, "We'll take a break for our sponsor here. Then we'll get back to Madeline Whelan in Honeydale, New York, who just won five _hundred_ thousand dollars in a jingle contest."

Maddy heard a hollow sound, then a voice that said, "Don't go away." She reached for Clark's hand. He pulled it away to pick up his magazine.

"Don't," she pleaded.

Rip Mangione was back on the line. "I'm talking with Madeline Whelan in Honeydale, New York, who just won five *hundred* thousand dollars in the Best-Buy Heavy-Duty Aluminum Foil jingle contest. Want to run the winning line by us, Madeline?"

"'Best-Buy Heavy-Duty Foil makes my life more beautifoil'" Her voice suddenly breathy and girlish, she added, "How's that for inspiration, Rip Mangione?" The talk-show host gave his appreciative laugh again. "Speaking of inspiration, what exactly did it for you, Madeline Whelan? I've got a lot of listeners who'd like to win five *hundred* thousand dollars."

She remembered it perfectly: Clark crooning his loving lullaby about beautiful, beautiful Maddy. She could hardly tell that to the world without seeming horribly boastful. "Oh, a little something my husband whispered in my ear," she improvised quickly.

Clark grunted, "Oh, my God," slapped his magazine down on the bed, and pulled on his shorts.

"All right, Madeline Whelan," Rip Mangione said enthusiastically. "So what does a housewife do when she wins five *hundred* thousand dollars?"

Maddy watched Clark stalk out of the room. "I'm buying my mother-in-law a house," she began, trying to focus on Anna Whelan's happiness.

"Better than having her live with you, is that right, Madeline Whelan? For those of you who just tuned in, Mrs. Whelan, a housewife from way up in Westchester County, New York, won five *hundred* thousand dollars in a jingle contest. Hey, I guess more people would enter those contests if they thought they could get rid of their mothers-in-law." Before the furious Maddy could get in so much as a word, he added, "Thanks for being with us, Madeline Whelan. Come spend some of that loot in sunny Miami." The line went dead.

Sitting frozen in disbelief, Maddy heard the crickets chirping. The sound was menacing now. There was so much night out there. Clouds had sailed in front of the moon, leaving the world in eerie darkness.

She heard Clark down in the kitchen, opening and closing the refrigerator door.

She dialed 1-305-555-1212 and asked the Miami operator for the number of radio station WMMM. Then she dialed that number.

"You have reached WMMM, the talk of Miami," a recorded voice said. "All our offices are closed now. Please call weekdays between—"

Hanging up, she got out of bed and pulled on Clark's candy-striped seersucker robe. She started down the stairs, then detoured by the girls' room. Nellie was sleeping peacefully, her arm around a three-legged pig, but Kendra was tossing in the throes of a heavy dream.

"It's all right, honey," she murmured, stroking red hair back from a damp brow, adjusting the sheet. "There's nothing to be afraid of. Mommy and Daddy are here."

Kendra wriggled, then seemed to drift off to a more peaceful place. Taking heart, Maddy went downstairs.

Clark was sitting in the den, a bottle of beer in his hand, looking at "The Tonight Show" with the sound turned down. He gestured at the place next to him on the convertible couch. "Sit down. You might get some ideas on what to wear when Carson has you on."

"Clark—"

Suddenly savage, he said, "I don't want the world knowing what I whisper in your ear, do you understand? If you'd rather talk to Miami than make love to me, that's your business, but leave me out of it."

"Dammit! *You* answered the phone. You could have said I was asleep, busy, anything."

"Oh, no." He thrust angry fingers back through his dark hair. "It wasn't my decision to make. It was yours."

"We'll get an unlisted phone," Maddy said, sitting down tentatively on the edge of the couch.

Looking unconvinced, Clark stared at the television screen. Carson was flapping his arms and laughing.

"We'll go to Venice," Maddy tried, "and Venice will be wonderful, and then we'll come back and be what we've always been."

"If we don't forget what that was," Clark said. He swallowed beer.

A chill running through her body, Maddy collapsed shivering into his arms. "Warm me, Clark," she cried.

His arms went around her. He held her tight. "Did you like being on the radio?" he couldn't help asking.

"Sort of. You know I like people. I liked thinking that for a minute I was part of hundreds of lives. Then Rip Mangione made a crack about mothers-in-law, and I could have throttled him."

"And me."

"Oh, you—" She gently pounded his shoulder with a fist. "I have better things to do to you."

"Show me."

"You'll have to take off your shorts," she said boldly. "And turn off Mr. Carson. And take the phone off the hook."

"Any other orders, ma'am?" He turned off the television set. He took the telephone off the hook, and put the receiver face down in a pillow to muffle the clicking sound.

"Enjoy."

Afterward he said he'd enjoyed, ever so much, and she said truthfully that she had too. But she went to sleep still feeling cold.

Chapter 6

M ADDY WHELAN LOVED CLARK WHELAN. She whispered the message into the briny air of Venice as they glided along the Grand Canal.

She had loved him in the warm clutter of their home, in the shrillness of the Olympus Diner, on the lush green roads of Westchester County; she had loved him everywhere they had been, and in every way. She had loved him absolutely, beyond measure, for ten years. Yet it was necessary—somehow necessary to all the world—that she love him here.

This shadow, that yielding archway, a narrow canal that invited you in and promised to get you lost, ancient windows that borrowed new gold from the melon sunset sky: They were all about her and Clark. Architects weaving lace out of stone five hundred years ago had somehow known they would be here today.

She leaned her head against his shoulder. Behind them, the gondolier's oar made a faint rhythmic music as it dipped into the shimmering apricot-stained water. No art history course had prepared her for the impact of the ancient buildings rising up out of the Grand Canal, as intricate and delicate as jewels, yet vast and massive. And no one— no parent or poet or self-appointed expert on relationships—had prepared her for the infinite richness and mysteriousness of love.

"Ca' d'Oro," the gondolier called out. "It means Golden House, though the gold is long gone. It is White House now," he went on in his charmingly accented English, "though very different from your White House, yes, signora?"

For a startling moment Maddy thought he was referring to the house in Honeydale where she and Clark lived. If Venice was a magic show, the gondoliers were its conjurers; it seemed quite within their power to visualize a place they'd never seen. But as she turned around to smile at the tall boatman, classically garbed in striped jersey and broad-brimmed straw hat, she realized he was referring, of course, to the Washington White House.

"*Sì, molto differente*," she said, loving the feel of Italian in her mouth. In just two days she'd developed a small command of some common phrases.

Indeed, the Ca' d'Oro *was* very different even from the other structures along the Grand Canal: pale, with three tiers of delicate columns lifting the eye through finely wrought open work to a crown of icing-like crenellation.

"*Bellissimo!*" she said to Clark, squeezing his hand.

"Hey, it's me, your good old American husband, remember?" he said. "The one who speaks English real good?"

Injured, she withdrew her hand and turned away to hide the sudden misting in her eyes. In the last two days she'd heard more sardonic comments from Clark than in the ten previous years. She'd tried telling herself it was jet lag, but the theory really didn't hold water. She knew Clark—body, mind, and soul; no mere assault on his body clock would remake his psyche.

She felt so privileged to be in Venice, so lucky to love him here. But she had no sense that he shared her feelings. Clark, the man who recited poetry to her while she hosed down the car or made a tuna-noodle casserole, seemed determined to be more everyday-than-thou as they bobbled on painted water past Byzantine splendors in the city of light.

A *motoscafo*, a slick blur of mahogany, sped by them, making waves. Maddy looked at the handful of passengers in the small boat, the women in brilliantly patterned silk dresses, the men in linen suits, laughing, taking pleasure in the night and one another. She wanted to jab Clark in the ribs and say: Look, that's how you honor Venice. You marvel in this stone bridge, at once curved and angular; in that unlikely pine tree. And you see the spark in each other; you love each other the more for being members of the species who put this heaven on earth. We can't build a Ca' d'Oro, you and I, but we have a genius for love. Our marriage is our Venice. A light for the world. We should be celebrating each other.

As the gondola bobbled, Clark said mirthlessly, "I think we hit a pothole. Just like being on our driveway."

Maddy searched desperately for a safe subject. "I can't wait to bring the girls here. When do you think they'll be the right age to really appreciate it?"

"I don't know. Why don't you bring them home some little memento—like the Doge's Palace—and see how they like it?"

"Gee," Maddy said, determined to be light, "I don't think we can quite afford to buy the palace yet. I'll have to win the Spring Run Bake-Off first."

"Don't underestimate your purchasing power." Looking at his watch, he said, "Back home, Dick Grable has just finished lunch, and he's working hard on making your money make money."

"*Our* money."

Clark gave her a look she'd been seeing too often in Venice, a look that was new to his repertoire—a half-smile, a narrowing of his gray eyes. Not exactly a cynical look, but a definite expression of doubt. "Our money," he echoed grudgingly.

"Rio della Maddalena," the gondolier said, pointing to a narrow canal.

"Madeline's River." Delighted, disbelieving, Maddy looked at the gondolier. His straw hat shadowed his face, making him unreadable. Did he know her name was Madeline? It seemed improbable, yet likely; this was a not quite ordinary man. Rio della Maddalena was hardly a point of major interest, like Ca' d'Oro or Accadémia or the Rialto Bridge. He must have known.

The gondolier feathered his oar and pointed the grand, gilded prow of his boat toward the small canal. He seemed also to know that Maddy had to explore the waterway that bore her name. As they turned off the Grand Canal, the shadows of evening deepened. Water slapped noisily at the pilings. Maddy felt the way she had as a child in funhouses at amusement parks—deliciously afraid.

The canal was so narrow that Maddy could feel a breath coming off the buildings to either side. She shivered against Clark, and his arm went around her; but it was a perfunctory move and did little to warm her. Still, she had no thought of asking the gondolier to turn back. Something was waiting for her, drawing her this way.

Though every stone spoke of centuries of history, she sensed there were no great monuments along this stretch; it felt like a neighborhood. She heard a child's tentative fingers on a piano, working at the Beethoven piece every child must play, "Für Elise." An unseen woman speaking a dialect Maddy could not understand was plainly calling the family to dinner. Somewhere a dog barked.

The canal veered to the left, then to the right.

"Here," the gondolier said. He drew the boat alongside a flight of steps and grabbed a striped pole.

Maddy and Clark exchanged looks. They'd hired the gondolier for an hour. He'd given them ten minutes more. But they'd expected to wind up back at the Gritti Palace, their hotel.

"You'll be happy here." The gondolier was grinning.

"How much to go back to the Gritti?" Clark asked.

Maddy tugged at his arm. She sensed that something was waiting for them. "No, let's get off here. We can always find our way back on foot or take the *vaporetto*. Anyway, I'm ready for a drink."

As they paid the gondolier, he said to Maddy, "My name is Bondini. When you need me again, just ask at the hotel."

"That man *knows* things," Maddy said to Clark as they climbed up the stone steps.

"You're not going to get mystical on me, are you? My down-to-earth Maddy?"

"You mean your boring suburban Maddy?"

Clark grabbed her so suddenly by the shoulders that she jumped; she could only think he'd seen a rat and was pulling her out of its path.

"Don't ever say that." His teeth were clenched; he shook her a little. "You're talking about the woman I've loved for ten years."

"She's not the only Maddy." Her voice was very small. "You've said so yourself. My wondrous contradictions, or something."

His hands dropped away from her; he looked at them as though in disbelief that they could have grabbed her, shook her. "Honey, I'm sorry," he said. "I'm sorry."

"It's all right," she said, meaning it; she was so relieved to hear him sound like the Clark she knew.

"You have every right to be fanciful, mystical, whatever," he said. "I just need to know that you haven't thrown away the other parts of yourself. Oh, Maddy, I need you to tell me you didn't spend ten years looking out the kitchen window hoping to be rescued from our life. From your everyday self."

"Listen," she said, taking his hand as they walked along the filled-in canal called the Rio Terra della Maddalena. "Do you remember what we used to say the year we were in college? That nothing in our lives would be absolute except each other—and now the girls, of course. When we had our degrees, we would spin the globe. Work in a poverty program here, teach there. I love our house and Honeydale and our friends. But I didn't marry them. I'm married only to you."

"Our home is a symbol of us," Clark said.

"Venice is a symbol of us," Maddy amended. When he didn't respond, she went on, her voice rising. "You're the one who kept telling me I had to enjoy our winnings, that anything else would be wrong."

His fingers tightened on her hand, as if she were a child who couldn't be trusted not to run away, but he didn't say anything. Maddy's smart Italian sandals—bought back at the Honeydale Mall at Clark's urging—made a pleasant slapping sound against the stone, almost filling the silence that hung between them. Almost.

They walked through a deserted *campo*. Maddy sensed that behind the thick walls surrounding them families were having dinner. She thought about Nellie and Kendra, as she did a hundred times a day. Were they at swimming lessons now, or archery, having the time of their lives—or were they sobbing out their homesickness against some counselor's chest?

JENNIFER ROSE

The street veered and brought sudden, blessed distraction: a Caffè Alla Maddalena. Maddy knew there must be a shrine to Mary Magdalene in these parts, but she couldn't help feeling stirred by the prevalence of what was also her name. Laughter rang out from the *caffè*, and they hurried toward it.

"Will you call me Maddalena now and then back home," she said lightly, "while I'm eating corned beef hash at the Olympus?"

"There won't be much hash from now on, I'm betting."

"Dammit, Clark!" she said, heating up. "You sound like Clem at the cleaners. I'm not going to change. I have it on no less authority than you."

"You've changed already."

She stopped dead still. "You're the one who's changed. Where's my lover, the man who romances me day and night?" Eyes fixed on him, she choked back a cry. In his blue-and-white-striped shirt and crisp white pants, he was the most familiar figure on earth. Yet suddenly she didn't know him as well as she knew Bondini the gondolier. "I wish I'd never entered the blasted contest," she heard herself blurt out. "I wish I'd left you with your debts and your nobility—"

"Nobility?"

"That's what hurts, isn't it? You won't any longer be saintly, self-sacrificing Clark Whelan making good his father's debts. Do you miss that weight on your shoulders? Are debts better than Venice?" Breaking away from him, she bolted for the *caffè* and sank into a chair at an outside table, howling into her hands.

"Maddy? Darling?" His voice hoarse with concern, Clark ran to her and gently pried her hands away.

She was crying; she was laughing. The laughter was winning. "Debts in Venice," she got out, between peals. "Isn't it wonderful? Shouldn't that win a contest? Thomas Mann's greatest unwritten novel, *Debts in Venice.*"

Clark's laughter was a roaring cleansing sound that seemed to come from the center of his being. "Maddy," he crooned, pulling his chair close to hers. "Maddy."

Maddy basked in the sudden rightness of the moment. Back home—if such emotional swings could have happened back home—

54

she would have died of embarrassment. But the people drinking aperitifs at the other tables didn't seem to mind. Maybe everyone had emotional cataclysms in Venice.

With a start, Maddy realized that the foursome at the next table were the elegant group who'd zoomed by them in a *motoscafo* on the Grand Canal.

"We have to stay for Redentore," one of the brightly dressed women was saying.

"Not if the *scirocco* hangs in," the other woman said. "It makes me too wicked." She laughed gaily.

A waitress came out. "Signore, signora?"

"*Punt e Mes, per favore,*" Maddy said, "*e un' acqua minerale.*"

Clark ordered a beer. "What's *Punt e Mes*?" he asked Maddy.

"An aperitif. I heard someone order it last night at Al Graspo de Ua, and I decided I'd try it today. I'm not going to have anything twice."

Apparently her voice had carried because one of the women at the next table called over, "I like your spirit, honey." She was a blonde in her late thirties or early forties, her hair scraped back to make much of the showy bones of her face. Maddy thought it must have taken her at least an hour to do her makeup. Her eyelids alone had three or four shades of green on them, darkest at the lash line and paling in gradations to a green-tinged white over the brow bone. Maddy felt bare-faced in the blusher and mauve eyeliner that had looked artful back at the hotel.

"But you have to have it on the rocks, or it's ghastly," the woman went on. "Like some horrible old cough medicine. Rocks, and a couple of twists." Not waiting for Maddy to say anything, she called to the waitress in rapid Italian, gesturing toward Maddy's and Clark's table. The drink came out with ice and two thin scrapings of lemon peel.

Maddy tasted it and raised her glass to the woman. "You're right," she called over. "It would be awfully cloying without ice." She wasn't sure it would ever be her favorite tipple even with ice, but its absolute newness pleased her. Back home she'd rarely drunk alcohol except for an occasional beer on very hot nights or a glass of dry white wine.

Clark sipped his beer in silence as Maddy and the two women chatted. Somehow the two tables merged. Names were exchanged.

The blonde and her husband were Kitty and Lyle Dunn. He had wavy silver hair and a commanding presence, and Maddy cast him as chairman of the board. The other couple were Justine Watters and Alex Emmerling. She had angular black hair, perfect red lips, and a habit of throwing back her head in silent laughter whenever she found someone witty. He was shorter than she, balding, and apparently held great charm for her. Maddy liked him, liked her for liking him.

She ordered another *Punt e Mes*. Two in one sitting was different from ordering the same thing twice.

Details spilled out into the warm, humid air. Kitty Dunn had spent her childhood summers in Venice, thus her fluent Italian. Lyle had just sold his printing business in Los Angeles, and maybe was, maybe wasn't, sorry. Justine had an art gallery in New York City, in Soho. And Alex wanted *panini*.

Maddy explained how she and Clark came to be in Venice. There was an explosion of delight.

"But I always thought those contests were fixed!" Justine exclaimed. "You're not the niece of the president of Best-Buy Products? You didn't sleep with one of the judges?"

Clark's beer went down the wrong way. As he gasped and sputtered, Justine threw her sculpted dark head back in silent laughter, as though he'd been awfully clever. The more practical Alex slapped him soundly on the back.

The waitress arrived with the *panini*, toasted little triangular sandwiches. Maddy tried one, a crusty savory filled with a sharp yet yielding melted cheese and a thin slice of vivid prosciutto. She thought it was delicious.

"No, thanks," Clark said heavily when the plate was offered to him. "We're going to dinner soon."

Maddy thought he sounded like a wound-up little boy whose mother had told him too often to be good, to wash his hands and face, and stay away from sweets. She ached for him. She ached for herself. He was saying no thanks to everything, to everyone, including—maybe most of all—herself.

The two couples may not have been people she wanted to spend her life with, but at least they knew the art of enjoyment. Aperitifs, sandwiches, words, and laughter seemed to fly around in a whirl of color, as if in some jazzy animated cartoon. Eagerly the four strangers pressed Maddy for details about the contest, and they relished every morsel of information she conveyed.

"It's a fairy tale," Kitty said on a rapturous sigh. "Honey, you're the American dream come true."

"Beautifoil." Alex slapped his knee. "Son of a gun. *Beautifoil.*"

"You must be very proud of her," Justine said to Clark.

"I am," Clark said stiffly. "She's a great mother, a great wife, an honest and generous woman. I've always been proud of her."

The banter came to a cold stop. Maddy shriveled inside. Lord, he'd done everything corny but call her a great American and a credit to her church. Somehow the two tables separated again. Maddy and Clark looked silently at each other until the waitress brought the bill.

They walked along narrow streets, not touching, still not talking. Maddy hoped they were lost. They deserved to be lost. But they saw an arrow for the San Marcuola *vaporetto* stop.

Waiting for the boat on the landing stage, they were surrounded by Venetians and tourists. It seemed to Maddy that everyone around them was happy: the Japanese family with the inevitable cameras; two Israelis who had just visited the sixteenth-century Jewish ghetto; a group of American college girls in jeans and sneakers; an old, black-garbed Italian woman carrying an enormous bag of fresh carrots.

Once upon a time she and Clark had been the happiest people she knew. Now a bag full of carrots seemed to elicit greater joy, to judge by the old woman's smiles, than he and she elicited from each other.

"I think we should go home," she finally said in a small, miserable voice.

"The *vaporetto* will be here any minute." Clark had jammed his hands into his pockets; his voice sounded jammed in, too.

"I don't mean home to the Gritti Palace. I mean home to Honeydale."

"You've got your appointment with Donatello tomorrow." He managed to make it sound like a distasteful rendezvous, if not downright illicit.

"That's in the morning. We could get a flight to Milan in the afternoon, then home."

"I'll go home," Clark said. "You like it here."

"I would love it here. If you let me love you here." The *vaporetto* was coming. More happy people. "Otherwise, it's nothing. So much stone."

Clark wouldn't let up. "You won't lack for company. If I hadn't been there to cramp your style, I'm sure you would have gone off to dinner with the wonderful people we met at the *caffè*."

"What was wrong with those people?" She raised her voice to be heard over the sound of the *vaporetto* arriving at the landing. The momentum of the crowd carried them forward in the boat.

"They were what you used to call the careless people." Hunching his shoulders against the breeze—or maybe against his inner misery—he went on, "I can just see Justine's gallery in Soho. Big canvases signifying nothing. Art that's in and out of fashion like clothes and restaurants. Kitty spends half her life getting dressed and painting her face, and the other half showing off the results."

"You don't know that," Maddy protested. A man in a leather jacket bumped her, purposely she thought, and she clutched her white shoulder bag closer to her.

"If they have children, they didn't mention them," Clark said.

"We didn't mention ours." The *vaporetto* stopped next at the Rialto landing. Looking at the carved stone of the bridge, Maddy couldn't believe that she and Clark were wasting the beauty of Venice the way they were, wasting each other.

Clark nodded triumphantly, his mouth as close to sneering as Maddy had ever seen it. "Exactly."

"Oh, Clark," Maddy all but exploded, "can't we go fifteen minutes without mentioning our children and not be terrible people?"

As though he didn't think the question needed answering, he said, "I very much had the feeling that Alex is married. And I don't mean to Justine."

"How on earth can you know that?" But she had to admit, at least to herself, that the same perception had come to her mind, too.

"We married men know each other." Clark laughed mirthlessly.

"Yes. But do you know yourselves?"

They got off at the Santa Maria del Giglio stop.

"I don't feel like going out to dinner," Clark said as they walked into the splendor of the Gritti Palace. "I'll order something in the room."

Maddy had never felt so shut out. "I'll have dinner in the restaurant here."

At the Terrazzo del Doge, they made a fuss over her, and she had a tender, tasty *osso buco*, though the texture of the marrow made her feel a little squeamish. But she had nothing to read except a guide book, and she was left to think a number of indigestible thoughts. She felt dreadfully self-conscious, even though this was her hotel and there were several other women dining alone. She realized, to her shock, that she had never before had dinner in a public place without Clark. Lunches, but always in modest places; and lunch was different, anyway.

A dark-haired, slimly built man in a dinner jacket tried to pick her up. Swiss, she thought; German Swiss. He didn't seem very fervent, and she wondered if he'd made the move just because he thought she looked sad.

When she went upstairs, the room was dark except for the small light on her side of the bed. Clark was asleep, or feigning sleep. She didn't care which. Her mind was numb. She didn't want talk. She wanted darkness, stillness, peace.

But her body had its own wants. She and Clark had always slept entwined the night through; at home they joked that their double bed was a waste except when they both were reading. She found it impossible to lie apart from him. His body was a magnet for hers.

She inched toward him, not wanting to wake him if he were sleeping, not wanting to concede anything if he were awake.

His arms encircled her. She still didn't know if he were conscious or not, still didn't care. He was there. Her Clark was there. Nothing else mattered for the night.

She felt a hand on her breast, giving and demanding at once, and an unmistakable hardness against her thigh. Dawn, she sensed blurrily; she could hear a suddenness of birds, the pigeons of the piazza. She didn't say a word, didn't open her eyes.

If she didn't quite wake up, she could pretend everything was all right.

He wasn't in a hurry; he wasn't quite awake, either, maybe. Don't look at him, don't talk, try not to think. Let the body make its own peace. Maybe the spirit would follow.

His fingers were kneading her nipples, her nipples needing his fingers. She wanted him to touch her hard, not minding if it hurt a little.

The hurt wasn't hurt. It got translated somehow. It was love; it couldn't hurt. A different brand of pleasure, that was all. Did other wives feel this way? She'd wanted to ask Jill, but she was shy. She could ask her new friend Kitty from Caffè Alla Maddalena. She could ask Bondini the gondolier. No secrets had been revealed in the place that bore her name, but never mind.

Both hands were on her breasts now, palms stroking, lips making a wordless murmur in her hair. Did he guess she was awake? He would let her play her game, the way she'd let him play his last night. One hand found its way between her thighs; oh. Oh.

The hand came back up along her belly, leaving her starving, jangling.

His tongue was on her ear, lazy, then madly ambitious for nectar. His tongue moved to her throat.

Maybe she only imagined she was awake, was playing at playing.

His hands were gently urging her to lie prone. His mouth was taking liberties with her back. Her spine became a river of lava as his lips sailed down.

He nipped at her buttocks. A punishment. A present. I am angry. I love you. I am angry. I love you.

Her thighs are not spared. He touched where she had them waxed, may her vanity be forgiven, to please his eye.

She felt kisses on the backs of the knees. No quarter was to be spared.

If she never opened her eyes, never spoke, the spell would last forever. It was a small price to pay for this joy. Love is not love that alters when it alterations finds. The marriage of true bodies is higher than a meeting of the minds.

There had been no message at the Maddalena. Or maybe this was the message—that there was no more important light in the world than the beacon of marriage.

His body was over her now, coming at her but not in her. His mouth was on her forehead, in her hair.

I am ready. Do not make me wait.

His mouth must first go everywhere, scorching the beaches, setting the lagoon on fire. I am Venice, and Venice is burning. I am as wide, as open, as the summer air.

He put himself inside her. Her shoulders rushed down to meet him; fiercely she claimed him everywhere.

The parts of the body fused in their hunger. "I love you." A separate hunger, a kind of glorious starvation because the words were so deeply felt but could not be said.

Fill me up, fill me up, fill me with love. Leave no room for anger and fear.

Claaark. Claaark. The first time in such a long time, though really it isn't so long, just feels like a small forever. Waves overlapping waves, don't lose me, don't let me die in this sea.

He was with her, and they were clinging, floating, keeping each other alive, never more alive.

She sighed, and his hands came around her again, but this time he was any old friendly, mortal husband, hugging her back to sleep.

Chapter 7

W HEN TRUE MORNING CAME, Maddy awoke to find Clark in a robe, sitting on a gilded chair looking out the window.

"Good morning," she called softly.

He turned to look at her. "Good morning."

She heard a tentativeness in his voice that had also been, she supposed, in her own. A slight embarrassment hung between them. It was as though they were strangers who had gone to bed together without learning each other's names. The clinging mist of exquisite intimacy only made the situation worse.

"What time is it?" she asked. A safe, neutral question. Next they could discuss the weather.

"Almost nine. Shall I order you some breakfast?"

Not *us; you.* His elaborate courteousness stung her more than rudeness would have done. This was her Clark, her husband, her lover, her love, being utterly impersonal.

"Let's go to Florian's," she said, trying to sound gay. They hadn't done so well at their last visit to a *caffè,* but almost anything would be better than staying locked in with each other and this mood. "We can watch the pigeons watch the tourists."

"You go ahead," he said. "I need a long walk."

She felt as though he'd tricked her, somehow. Her stomach churned. "Will you meet me at Donatello's's?" She cursed herself for her begging tone, then cursed herself again for caring how she sounded. This was *Clark* she was talking to, her soulmate of ten years' standing. How could she possibly be self-conscious?

"You don't need me at Donatello's."

I do, she wanted to cry. I need you everywhere. Drawing breath, she couldn't stop herself from saying softly, "I always thought you cared more about my clothes than I did."

Her words seemed to loosen him. His shoulders lost their stiffness, his face its frightening impassivity. "I always thought so, too. But right now I'm afraid I'd just cramp your style." He made a broad gesture encompassing the luxurious view, the terrace bar and Grand Canal below, maybe Venice and all the rest of Europe.

Maddy leaned back against the crispness of her pillow. "You *are* my style," she insisted. "You're the man who always made me feel like Myrna Loy to your William Powell. You turned the Olympus Diner into a four-star restaurant with anemones on every table. You had a way of making me feel romantic even when the kids were sick and I was changing puked-on sheets in the middle of the night."

"I know," Clark said calmly. He was smiling now, but sadly. "Here it's a different story, though. You don't need me here, Maddy. Everyone and everything is romantic. I don't feel like William Powell. I feel like a Westchester County florist."

"It's not what you do that matters, it's what you *are*."

"Yesterday when we were talking with your charming new friends," Clark said, "I was what I was—and succeeding in turning you and everyone else off."

Maddy couldn't hold back a tiny grimace. "You did lay it on awfully thick."

"You mean I was too corny?" His voice held a note of bitter triumph. "A quality you used to rather like in me."

There was a shout from below, on the Grand Canal; not a shout of anger or disaster, but someone's surprise and joy. It was the sort of sound she and Clark should be making, the sort of sound they'd often made in the past, as they'd turned any old everyday corner and found themselves face to face with a sudden reminder of the secret sweetness of life. How painfully far they seemed from such moments.

"It wasn't the corniness," she said. "It was your making me sound so saintly. I'm not that good. I'm not that simple. I don't want to have to be." She swung her long legs out of bed, as though to emphasize her point. Clark had more than once lovingly called them wicked legs.

"I'm going to have a shower," she said. "Then dress. I'll have a coffee and something flagrantly sweet at Florian's. Then I'm going to keep my appointment with Donatello. After that I want to go inside St. Mark's. Do you want to join me for any or all of the above?" Holding her breath, she felt a fierce nostalgia for the Clark who would say, "Let's start with the shower, darling." But he did not surface.

"I'll meet you in front of St. Mark's," Clark said quietly. "One o'clock? One-thirty?"

"One," Maddy said. She wanted him to know how eager she was to get past this moment, to be in a different place with him.

Suddenly there seemed to be no more to say, and she padded silently into the bathroom, avoiding Clark's eyes as she passed him. She ran the shower as hard as she could, creating a narrow world of sound and sensation, numbing herself.

Any moment the film called *Clark and Maddy* would dissolve abruptly to a scene of reconciliation, laughter swelling over the sound track. "How foolish we were," they would murmur to each other. Their love stronger than ever, they would step into Bondini's gondola and float into the sunset.

Sighing, Maddy stepped out of the shower and wrapped herself in the luxurious swath of terrycloth toweling that the hotel provided. She went to the gleaming basin and scrubbed her teeth. She got out her plastic travel bottle of Mother Earth Cucumber Moisturizer and the sheer foundation she wore, but the mirror was too steamy to use. She lifted a face towel to wipe it clean, then thought better of the act. Putting her forefinger to the mirror, she drew a heart. Inside it, she wrote: MW xxx CW.

A bubble seemed to burst inside her chest. Suddenly she couldn't stand the pain of estrangement from Clark. She pulled open the bathroom door, calling his name.

But he was gone—having dressed hastily, to judge from the robe uncharacteristically dropped on a chair. She found a note scribbled on a piece of the fine airmail-weight hotel stationery:

Darling,
    We *will* get through this. I'm off to wherever my feet want to take me. Have a really good time at Donatello's. See you at the basilica.

Much love,
Clark

She stood there clutching the note to her breast, staring vaguely out at the terrace bar and the brilliant blue of the Grand Canal. It was a lovely note, and he'd only meant well, of course. He couldn't have foreseen the terrible anxiety flaring up inside her. A foolish—but unstoppable—collage of disasters flashed in front of her eyes: Clark getting lost in a maze of dark, twisting alleys; Clark falling into a canal; Clark (the innocent, the trusting, the unabashed tourist) getting mugged; Clark stopping for lunch at some excessively humble spot and carelessly drinking the local water.

Clark and Maddy turning out not to be a comedy. No happy ending, after all.

"Oh, Maddy," she chided herself softly, "this isn't like you." Then again, she told herself, it wasn't like Clark simply to wander off.

With a little start she realized how much comfort she'd derived over the past ten years from nearly always knowing exactly where he was. When Kendra had been stung by a wasp, when her car had broken down on the Saw Mill River Parkway, she'd needed only one quick call to reach him. At moments when she simply wanted to visualize him, she'd known what background to set him against. He wasn't only her lover, her companion, her pal; he was also her safety net.

And she had always been his. Her heart had a moment of recognition. Maybe his strangeness in Venice came down to this: He needed to know who she was, just as she, unconsciously, had always needed to know where he was.

But—dammit!—she wasn't denying him knowledge of herself. If anything, the opposite was true. She was trying to show him her many selves, trying to evoke a Clark to dance with every Maddy. Surely he was as multifaceted as she was.

Enough of this fruitless thinking. She threw all her concentration into choosing her clothing for the day, beginning with panty stockings and a conservative but lush ivory satin slip. Surveying her modest array of clothing in the very big closet, she had to smile. Obviously the typical guest at the Gritti Palace didn't travel quite so lightly.

She chose a gray crinkled cotton suit with a fashionably big silhouette and long, loose lines, and a silvery silk blouse. It seemed an eternity ago that she'd bought it. She'd needed something to wear for the luncheon at which the chairman of the board of Best-Buy would hand her a check for five hundred thousand dollars. Unwilling to spend money she couldn't quite believe would be hers, she'd gone to her usual discount store. If Jill hadn't been there with her, she wouldn't have bought this suit, even at a discount.

After the presentation lunch, and after watching thirty seconds of herself on the six o'clock news as Nellie and Kendra shrieked, she'd been glad about the suit. She was glad now, too, she decided, slipping her feet into flawless red pumps. Impulsively she tied Donatello's red and silver scarf to her red shoulder bag.

She tried telling herself she was dressing to meet Clark, but honesty prevailed. She wanted Donatello to think well of her. Was that so shameful?

An hour and a half later, as she approached the building she'd been directed to, her confidence flagged. She'd seen luxury shops all over Venice, but this was no mere shop. Her letter of instruction had told her only to go to the Campo Quercia in the Dorsoduro quarter. It had said nothing of a magnificent eighteenth-century palace.

Staring awestruck at the rosy sweep of stone, Maddy decided she must have read the signs wrong. Surely this splendid structure, protected by iron gates, was a museum of some sort, or perhaps a consulate. No; a discreet brass plate set in the gate said DONATELLO.

The gate was locked; she pressed a button. A soft electronic buzz, very twentieth century, let her know she could push the gate open. Was there a hidden camera somewhere that had inspected her? Or had she rung the bell with the unmistakable authority of a woman dressed by great designers?

She crossed a courtyard in which marble men and women were grouped beneath intensely green trees with red blossoms, an eternal garden party. The courtyard wrapped itself around the palace, edging toward the Grand Canal.

A flight of stone stairs beckoned. At the top a door was opened by a butler in tails. Maddy had never seen a real live butler before; a giggle rose in her throat. Her mind raced into the past future tense. "A butler!" she was telling Jill over ice cream somewhere in Honeydale Center. "Dressed just like Jeeves!"

"*Buon giorno,*" she greeted him. "*Sono la Signora Whelan.*"

Though she had no doubt he spoke far better English than he did Italian, he courteously replied to her in the latter language, asking her to come in. She found herself in one of the most stunning rooms she had ever seen. The vaulted ceilings had to be twenty-five feet tall. The walls were hung with rich, intricate tapestries in which red and silver predominated. A soft light filtered in through leaded windows overlooking the courtyard. As though to keep the room from being too solemn, too unrelievedly splendid, cherubs winked down at her.

As the butler led her through a doorway, she realized the first room had been only a foyer. Now she found herself in a room that dwarfed a concert-size grand piano. Huge modern canvases on the wall—she recognized a Miró and a Dubuffet—beautifully exploited the scale. Underneath her feet exotic Peking carpets sprang to meet her. Smoked mirrors returned a tenderly distorted version of her face.

"Oh!" she exclaimed, catching sight of a chair. She had no Italian with which to answer the butler's grave look at inquiry. Gesturing to her scarf and to the fabric covering the chair, she said, "They are the same."

"*Sì, signora,*" he said, courteous, indifferent, leaving Maddy with the discomfitting feeling that she somehow shouldn't have spoken.

Shouldn't have? an interior voice retorted. According to what absurd protocol? People were people, whether they were princes or butlers. Probably the butler had more interesting things to say than Donatello.

She was formulating a comment about the glorious weather—not profound, but all that her Italian was up to—when a tall, dark-haired woman entered the room. Maddy all but heard the energy crackle as she stretched out a hand in welcome.

"Mrs. Whelan? I am Elena Maggiore, Donatello's assistant." Her English was flawless, with a British intonation. Shaking Maddy's hand, she gave a little gasp and tilted her head to one side. "But you are beautiful!" she exclaimed. "Stunning! We were expecting the woman in the photograph."

"Photograph?" Maddy echoed, confused.

Elena Maggiore took Maddy by the elbow. "You know—of that clever thing you do with the aluminum foil and your sink. In the photograph it was your typical American housewife. Cute, but—" She made a sweeping gesture with her free arm, as though the end of the sentence were, "—but nothing to do with all this." Taking a look at Maddy's face, she burst out laughing. "Oh, no. She is your sister?"

"My best friend," Maddy said quietly. "If she hadn't posed for that photograph, I probably wouldn't have won the contest."

"Loyal!" A look of amusement on her starkly beautiful face, Elena guided Maddy toward the door. "A quality we prize in Venice. You are enjoying our city?"

They were walking down a long corridor. Off to the right Maddy saw a kitchen from another era, with whitewashed walls, an open hearth, and a huge marble table. Maddy thought of the small marble pastry slab she had at home for rolling out her pie crusts. She wanted that table.

"I love Venice," she said. "Everything's larger than life—but then life is larger than life, isn't it?"

Elena Maggiore clapped her meticulously manicured hands. "*Brava!* You are truly a Venetian spirit. I think it was ordained that you win the contest."

"How did Signore Donatello come to be involved with the contest?" Maddy asked. "It's something I've been wondering."

The question earned her a quizzical look. "But it's a natural, isn't it?" Elena answered quickly. "What city shimmers with light, what city is beautifcil? Venice. Only Venice. And once you have Venice, you have Donatello. It's that simple."

Was it that simple? Something in the other woman's voice made Maddy uncertain. There was a question that begged to be asked—but what was it? If only Clark were there.

Now they were in a room that had a very different feeling from the others. Sketches of fantastical clothes, blown up to poster size, adorned the walls. A few dresses hung from hand-carved trees with fanciful branches. A silk suit was draped with studied casualness over a pink velvet settee. There was a double bed made up with wildly patterned silk sheets, rumpled by an artful hand, with a beautifully clashing nightgown and peignoir flung across it. This was obviously the boudoir of a rich, gorgeous, narcissistic woman who wore nothing but Donatello clothes. Except that it wasn't a boudoir, of course; it was his boutique.

All questions fled Maddy's mind as she looked around, frankly gaping. For the first time she understood why some women she knew would hock their souls for great clothes. To adorn oneself in Donatello's silk would be to put on a magic cloak. Here were colors, she thought, that had never existed before on earth. They had been stolen from the wildness of the sunset, from the strangest reaches of the sea.

"I think my art is not wasted on you," a resonant voice said beside her.

She turned to see the man who had to be Donatello. Younger than she'd expected—not more than twenty-five—he was about her height and as slim. Dark eyes flashed in a tanned face. His cheekbones were high, his mouth playful. Dressed in a double-breasted dark suit, impeccable white shirt, and rainbow-hued silk tie, he was, she supposed, the pluperfect Venetian male. There was just one surprising note, but she could hardly consider it a flaw. He had burnished red hair startlingly like her own.

"I never knew until today that clothing *was* an art," she said.

"Rarely is it," Donatello said in honeyed tones. Like Elena Maggiore, he spoke nearly perfect English, but his cadences and his arrangement of words had a definite, delicious Italian hue. His liquid eyes assessed her suit in an appraisal taking all of twenty seconds. "Take what you are wearing. It's stylish, it flatters, it is what one calls *good*. But does it expand your idea of the *possible*? My critics have called my clothes too costume-like, but we need costumes, for we are all actors and actresses playing many roles."

Maddy caught her breath. "But that's so very close to what I believe!" she exclaimed.

Donatello laughed, flipping back hair not only her color but also nearly as long as hers. "And you are amazed we speak the same language, Signora Whelan. You are an inverse snob, I think. You do not believe anyone with a palace can have important thoughts." Suddenly fluttering around her, his hands reminding her of birds in flight, he said, "But has no one offered you refreshment? Elena! Please tell Paolo we must have an *ombretta*."

When the butler appeared with a bottle of wine in a silver bucket, Maddy wanted wanted to protest that she never drank during the day. But Donatello forestalled her polite phrases.

"You cannot know Venice unless you know the custom of the *ombra*." He pointed to tiny goblets scarcely bigger than cordial size. "A very small glass of wine, to spark the senses, not dull them. Come. You have never tried Cartizze, no?"

"But this is extraordinary," Maddy proclaimed, almost humming after one small sip. "Like champagne, but it doesn't tickle the nose."

Donatello roared. "Signora Whelan, how well you play the innocent American housewife. It is a satisfying role?"

Maddy took another sip from her miniature glass. She felt the wine had not been made by men; it had bubbled up out of the earth in a crystalline spring. In the back of her throat she tasted wildflowers. "The most satisfying role I can imagine," she said. Emboldened by the amazing wine, she went on, "Perhaps I like that role best because I play it best. Marriage and motherhood are my art."

"And you are good?" Donatello looked at her almost angrily. "You are as good as I am at mine?"

Elena leaned forward, as though to shield Maddy, but Maddy just smiled.

"I'm pretty good," she said. She thought of Clark wandering the maze of Venice; she thought of Nellie and Kendra at camp—were they scared of the water, as she'd been at that age? She wasn't perfect, but no artist was perfect. Picasso had torn up many canvases. "I'm pretty good."

"No one has just one art," Donatello retorted.

Maddy looked around the room. "You have another talent as big as this?"

"Ask Elena," he said, and laughed.

Elena flushed, and Maddy felt her own color grow high. She retreated to the future again, telling Jill everything, line for line. "Well, that's what you were there for," she imagined Jill saying in her earthy way. "You would have been crushed if he'd turned out to talk like someone at a PTA meeting."

Maddy heard the ringing of sweet chimes, the opening of doors. Paolo, the butler, announced that a Signorina Cezeska had arrived. A tingle raced up Maddy's spine. Could it possibly be Elzbieta Cezeska, the great Polish actress? Movie buff that she was, Maddy had seen several of her films. Now there was someone who had many sides and knew how to honor them all.

When she saw the Twiggy-like face, the blunt-cut blond hair, and a figure that was bosomy, leggy, and gaminelike all at once, she knew she had guessed right. Donatello, obviously an old friend, greeted the actress with a warm embrace.

Introducing the actress and Maddy to each other, he explained about the jingle contest. The actress's delicate features became a frieze of delight.

"But it's a movie!" she exclaimed.

"With costumes by Donatello!" the designer added immediately. He poured the actress an *ombra*.

"Starring La Cezeska," Elena said. Then, putting a hand on Maddy's arm, she added, "Do you need an agent, Signora Whelan? Any moment they will try to buy the rights to the story of your life."

Donatello snapped his fingers. "Alex," he said, with the look of a man who has just been struck by inspiration.

"Alex?" drawled Elzbieta Cezeska, crossing flawlessly sculpted legs. Maddy tried to memorize each intonation, each gesture, to tell to Clark and then Jill.

"Alex Emmerling," Donatello said. "He is here on a little vacation, but is Alex ever on vacation? I am sure he is looking for a property. But Signora Whelan," he said abruptly, his hands in flight again, "I cannot bear it another moment. Off with your clothes."

Maddy's eyes got hot. She knew she was smiling dumbly.

"You are too beautiful for gray, however much it is the color of the moment. I must see you in Donatello." The designer bounded across the room to one of his fanciful wooden trees. Unceremoniously peeling a dress from a hanger, he held it up against Maddy; no, he flung it at her, she thought.

"I met Alex Emmerling last night," she said, trying to recover her composure. "At the Caffè Alla Maddalena. He was going on about the *panini.*"

Everyone laughed knowingly, and Elena said, "He lives to eat, that one."

Donatello was deflected for a moment. "Yes, this is for you," he said of his dress. "I must see you in it at once."

Maddy stared at the blaze of electric greens, edible yellows, and the red-orange-pink of a freshly sliced peach. "But does it fit?" she stammered.

"Fit?" Donatello looked as though she had uttered an obscenity. "But am I not known for exactly this? That my clothes fit everyone who should wear them? Look here," he said, showing Maddy how the shoulders merely tied. "And the skirt is to wear tight, loose, however it falls. The hem is irregular, so how does it matter? *That* is my triumph, Signora Whelan, not only my magnificent fabrics. You, Elena, Elzbieta, the Princess of Wales—you all can wear this dress. And you are very different women, no?" Spinning around as he talked, he sank into his seat, then sprung up again. "You are uncomfortable taking off your clothes in front of us all, my American friend?" he asked with a grin. "Can you not think of me as a doctor?"

"Oh, do leave her alone," Elzbieta Cezeska cried. "It's not as if you didn't have a dressing room."

Maddy shot her a grateful look. Elena Maggiore seemed galvanized into at least token sisterliness. "Come," the stunning dark-haired woman said. Leading Maddy to a dressing room nearly as big as the Whelans' master bedroom back in Honeydale, she discreetly drew a curtain made of streamers of Donatello silk.

As Maddy stepped out of her suit skirt, she thought that, really, she had been rather a prude. The ivory satin slip she was wearing covered a good deal more of her skin than the bikini she wore at the beach back home. Then again, she'd always thought a bikini mostly revealed that she didn't have much to reveal—at least in the bosom department.

"Can you not think of me as a doctor?" she asked her mirrored image. "But you don't look at me the way a doctor does," she retorted. It wasn't until she said the words that she realized they were true. When Dr. Carpenter, who'd delivered the twins, examined her, he was looking at parts, and looking at them with such clinical detachment that Maddy felt detached from them herself and could discuss them with ease.

Donatello looked at all of her—not just her body, but her essence as well. The more layers she wore in front of him, the better!

But meanwhile, the dress! Tugging here, wrapping there, she felt as if she'd plucked a rainbow from the sky and were clothing herself in it. She had never before been quite so pleased with her physical self.

From the smiles she saw when she stepped out of the dressing room, the pleasure wasn't just hers.

"You know," she blurted out, "I think this is a generous dress. It gives to me, and it makes me feel I'm giving to everyone else." She twirled around, as excited as the twins were when they dressed for a party.

"*Sì generoso*," Donatello roared, looking as though he might explode with delight. "This is the woman I have been waiting for." Shaking his head sadly, he said, "American women have not understood me. You will be my liaison to them. Signora Whelan, you are my Lady Luck."

Maddy couldn't help noticing that Elzbieta Cezeska and Elena Maggiore exchanged nervous looks. Was she threatening them somehow?

Donatello jumped up. "Come. We must go to Harry's Bar for lunch. All of us. To celebrate."

"I can't, my love," the actress said. "I have an appointment." She smiled mysteriously, and Maddy thought she had never seen a more expressive face.

"And I'm meeting my husband," Maddy said. Glancing at her watch, she added, "I ought to leave in a few minutes, in fact. I have to be at the basilica at San Marco at one."

"You will go in my *motoscafo*," Donatello said. "And you will collect your husband and meet us at Harry's Bar. The basilica has been here nearly a thousand years. It will wait a few hours for your visit. Yes, I must meet the man fortunate enough to be your mate." Giving Maddy no time to reply, he suddenly grabbed a six-foot-long scarf and wound it once around Elzbieta Cezeska's throat. The ends floated down over the loose Donatello blouse she wore with a wide white skirt. Maddy gasped at the effect. The greens of the blouse turned into shadowy pools underneath the sheer blues of the scarf.

"A present," Donatello said to the actress. "Because this is a great day."

"With you it's always a great day," Elzbieta said, embracing him.

Why, he's a good man, Maddy thought. A *good* man. He'll like Clark, and Clark will like him.

Meanwhile, she mustn't be late. Clark was never late. She started back toward the dressing room, where she had left her suit.

"But no," Donatello said, a hint of impatience in his voice. "From now on you wear only my things. To sleep, to swim, to play golf . . ."

"I don't play golf," Maddy said. "I drive in carpools, I bake, I sell vitamins and natural cosmetics."

Donatello's laughter rang out again. "So very, very American," he said. "And yet her soul is Venetian. I cannot believe my luck. For you, my beautiful signora, there will be carpool dresses. A divided skirt is the thing for driving, no? And aprons for when you bake."

"Machine-washable?" Maddy asked, daring.

"Yes, yes, yes, and in the machine to dry. You want potholders? There will be potholders."

Maddy shook her head, disbelieving. "All because I won the contest?"

Donatello gestured away that idea. "Of course not, *bella*. Had you been the woman I was expecting, three or four dresses, some swim wear, a nightgown and robe, a scarf or two. A handshake, hello, and good-bye."

"How did you get involved with the contest, anyway?" Maddy asked.

The loquacious designer suddenly fell silent. "Oh, it's a boring story," he finally said. Glancing at his watch, he went on, "It's time to get you into the *motoscafo.*"

Chapter 8

S t. Mark's Basilica was a dream of golden spires against a blameless sky.

Maddy had seen the renowned church perhaps a dozen times now. Yet it awed her as it had on the first glimpse; it would awe her if she lived in Venice and saw the basilica every day. Eastern and Western, Byzantine, Gothic, and Renaissance all at once, it did fabulous honor to her favorite notion: the infinite complexity of life. Though her formal religious faith was most at home in a simple white wooden church on the edge of the Honeydale Green, her mind leaped to meet the minds that had built San Marco. There was only one God, and God was the only one; everything else was many.

Hundreds of Venetians and tourists were sharing the moment with her. But where was Clark? The two bronze figures atop the Clock Tower had struck the hour. Raising her hand to her forehead as a shield against the brilliance of the day, she scanned the crowd in every direction. There were other American men in striped shirts with rolled-up sleeves and cuffed khaki pants, but not her man. Her earlier anxieties surfaced again. It just wasn't like him to be late.

On top of her anxiety, she was more than a little self-conscious.

Although Venetians were known for their fanciful dress, and bright colors abounded in the piazza, she was attracting a number of stares. Though they were admiring, she felt uncomfortable. She must look like someone who wanted to be on display.

But didn't she want to be? She tried to conjure up the feeling she'd had when she first put on Donatello's rainbow dress, the feeling that to wear it was to give. She tried smiling back at the smiles, without making her smile a "yes." That was better than just standing there, but not much.

Where was Clark, dammit? They had agreed on one o'clock, hadn't they? Right here, in front of St. Mark's? Or had it been one-thirty, back at the Gritti Palace? No, she was right on time and in the right place.

"*Bellissima!*" a voice whispered behind her.

Trying to make her movements casual, she took a step forward.

"*Bellissima!*" the voice said again, with even more enthusiasm, its owner staying with her.

Out of the corner of her eye, she had a glimpse of blond hair and smoldering eyes.

Damn! She should have stayed in her ladylike cool gray suit.

Not wanting to leave the area where she was supposed to meet Clark, but anxious to escape the insinuating voice and, she suspected, eager hands, she took a few steps toward a large group. A guide with a definite Australian inflection was loudly declaiming to his charges on the virtues of the portal mosaics. Maddy would surely lose her admirer there.

"And on the left, we have a mosaic showing the Venetians carrying the body of Saint Mark into the church," the guide was saying robustly. "This is the oldest mosaic on the façade. It dates from around 1265."

"What month in 1265?" one of his group called out, evoking laughter from the others. Evidently the guide had not been stinting on dates.

"*Bellissima!*" came the hoarse whisper again. "*Mi piace molto.*"

She groaned inwardly. She might please him, but he didn't please her. Well, there was no point in closing her eyes and hoping he would just go away. She turned around, and in her coolest, most dismissive voice, said simply, "*Non sono interessante.*"

To her amazement and dismay, he burst out laughing. "*Sì, signora,*" he said caressingly. "*Lei e molto interessante.*" Coming a step closer, he looked as if he were considering lunching on various parts of her anatomy.

Though it was broad daylight in a richly populated public space, Maddy felt afraid. No, not afraid, her mind corrected itself; she felt as if she'd already been assaulted. Back home she'd always taken smiles from strange men in stride. Even the occasional wolf whistle had seemed harmless enough, merely an acknowledgment that she'd brightened someone's day.

This man's attentions felt different, though. Maybe because in the sensuous swirl of Donatello's dress she must have seemed to invite attention? Dammit! If only she could get away from the man. But she couldn't take a chance on missing Clark. Oh, why had he chosen today to be late?

At a loss for another phrase of dismissal, she said even more firmly, "*Signore, non sono interesante.*"

Again came laughter, a shaking of the head, an indication that he wasn't the least bit discouraged.

A tall, very thin man with gray hair broke away from the Australian group. "Look here," he said to Maddy, "I couldn't help listening. I gather you were trying to tell him that you're not interested. But you've been telling him that you're not interesting."

Maddy clapped her hand over her mouth, but a bubble of laughter surfaced anyway. "Oh, no," she said. "The poor, confused man. Could you possibly say the properly discouraging thing? Obviously, your Italian's a lot better than mine."

A few rapid-fire words from the tall Australian, and the other man turned without a word and walked away.

Maddy regarded her rescuer with amazement. "What on earth did you tell him? That I'm a spy for the CIA?"

"Certainly not. That would just have inflamed him. I told him that you have a very jealous husband . . . who carries a knife. I hope it's not true because our guide is destroying Venice for me, and I'd like to escape for a coffee. With you. Do you favor Florian's or Quadri?" A gentle smile lit the man's bony face.

"The knife part isn't true, and he's never had occasion to be jealous, but I do have a husband," Maddy said. "I'm supposed—oh, there he is. Thank heaven! Clark!"

"Hello, darling. Sorry I'm late." Clark brushed a kiss across her mouth.

He was the Clark of old, Clark as played by William Powell or Cary Grant, not the stranger she'd woken up with that morning. Maddy looked at him wonderingly. Had some magical corner of Venice cured him of his unhappiness with her? Or was he perhaps performing for the thin man from Australia and everyone else in the square? If the world thought they were the great romance, they would *be* the great romance. It was a tempting lure.

Meanwhile, the Australian was standing there as his guide carried on about the mosaic over the middle portal, a Last Judgment done in 1836.

Taking Clark's left hand, she said, "Darling, this nice man just rescued me from someone who was being a little too attentive. This is my husband, Clark Whelan. And I'm Madeline Whelan." She paused expectantly.

Instead of offering his name, the man exclaimed delightedly, "Madeline Whelan of Honeydale, New York? Madeline Whelan who won five hundred thousand dollars?" Lowering his voice, he added, "I'm Ian Pargetter."

Now it was Maddy's turn to gape. Ian Pargetter was the man invariably described as "the other newspaper baron from Down Under." The owner of dozens of papers in Australia, Great Britain, Canada, and the United States, he was said to have enormous influence on the day-to-day thoughts of the English-speaking world.

As she offered her hand, she said, "What are you doing with a tour group? I thought you traveled everywhere in your own plane."

"Oh, yes, the Big Kangaroo is sitting out at Marco Polo Airport," he said, as casual as if he'd been talking about a car, not a DC-8. "But I started out as a reporter, and I still like to keep my hand in. The organizers of this tour rake in millions of pounds annually from hardworking Australians. I thought I'd tag along incognito for a few days and write a story on whether people are getting their money's worth." He winked broadly. "Don't give me away."

"How do you know about me?" Maddy blurted out, awed by the realization that she was casually chatting with one of the most powerful men on earth.

She felt Clark stiffen at her side. "Mr. Pargetter must read his own papers. He owns *The Banner*, you know. You remember that story, don't you, darling? The one about the Madeline Whelan who slams doors in people's faces?"

"Oh," Maddy said in a small voice.

"Never mind," Ian Pargetter said brashly. "People read *The Banner* for entertainment, not truth."

"I suppose I should have talked to the reporter for a few minutes." Maddy wished Clark would stop giving her such ferocious looks.

The Australian publisher shrugged. "She'd have gotten it wrong, no doubt," he said. The idea didn't seem to perturb him in the least. "What we need is for a real journalist to interview you. Myself, for instance. People are awfully curious about what happens to contest winners. Did you get champagne on your flight? Were there flowers waiting for you in your hotel room? Is all of Venice at your feet? And what does it all feel like . . . for both of you?" Looking from one to the other, he said, "Yes, I've not doubt there's a real story here. Can I buy the two of you lunch? If I have lunch with my guide, he'll probably try telling me the age of whatever I eat. *Sono molto interessante*," he added engagingly.

Laughing, Maddy explained the joke to Clark. He didn't laugh.

"We've got a lunch appointment," he said before Maddy could respond to the invitation. "We're late as it is." With no attempt at softening the curt refusal, he put pressure on Maddy's arm and started to lead her away.

Maddy was furious, but she wasn't about to air her feelings in front of a stranger. As if he sensed her predicament and wanted to save her from embarrassment, Ian Pargetter gave a small wave of his hand and started back toward his group.

"I'm at the Bauer Grünwald if you want me," he said. With a sigh, he turned his attention to the tour guide.

"The upper arch mosaics were started in 1385 . . ."

"We'll have to come back to the basilica later," Clark said through clenched teeth. "I said we had a lunch appointment." He steered Maddy toward the western end of the piazza.

"We do have a lunch appointment," Maddy said coldly. "Donatello invited us to join him at Harry's Bar, and I accepted. The basilica has been there a thousand years. It'll wait a few hours for us to see it."

"That line comes straight from the great Donatello, no doubt," Clark said with a dark smile. "Typical of the brittle sort of things your new friends say."

"Oh, honestly, Clark!" Maddy angrily shook off his hand. "You'd think I'd taken up with a gang of criminals. They're not my friends, but they happen to be interesting acquaintances. And nice, too. When Ian Pargetter rescued me from that man, I was within an inch of getting pinched."

Clark started moving at a faster pace, as though to put distance between himself and the Australian. "What do you expect men to do when you dress like that? Honestly, Maddy, you're a walking invitation."

"I am not!" she replied indignantly, forgetting that the thought had crossed her own mind not long before. "Mostly this dress just makes people smile. Everyone but you," she added, turning away in hopes of forestalling tears.

"It's gorgeous," Clark said grimly.

"Well, we don't all have to dress like preppies, do we?" she cried in a rush. "Just because you only feel at home in striped shirts and khakis doesn't mean the rest of us have to be constricted."

"This is a checked shirt," he said.

"Oh, don't be technical. You know what I mean. Did it ever occur to you that I might like to see you in something different?"

Clark said nothing for a moment. Then: "No, it didn't. I never thought my clothes were such a big deal for you. Or that yours were. Or anyone's."

"Clothing can be an art, too." Maddy's mind felt like a kitten chasing its own tail. Words kept forming on her lips, and only afterward registering on her brain.

"Great," Clark said. "Another Donatello line, I bet." He stopped stock still. "Why am I going to this lunch, anyway?"

"Because I want you there," Maddy said in a small voice.

"Do you?" He crooked a finger under her chin and forced her eyes to meet his. "In my checked shirt, and all?"

Maddy nodded.

As the crowd flowed around them, Clark put gentle fingers on the rainbow silk fluttering freely over Maddy's bosom. "I do actually like this dress," he said. "I apologize for saying you invited that lecher. It never would have happened if I had been there. It was my fault for being late."

"I was worried about you." Maddy leaned against his chest, shuddering with relief as his strong arms closed around her. "I'm not used to not knowing where you are. And you're never late."

"I'm sorry," he said, but he didn't explain. "I never want to make you worry."

"And I'm sorry for—" Her words hung in the air. "Being difficult for you. But I do think," she went on, almost in spite of herself, "that you were very tough on Ian Pargetter. It's not as if the *Banner* story destroyed me."

"You mean you would have liked him to interview you," Clark said. His broad brow furrowed, as if in pain.

They turned onto the Calle Vallaresso.

"No, but I did owe him thanks. And we both owed him common courtesy."

"Did we?" Clark shook his head. "In the old days you would have loved my loyalty to you. You would have looked up at me with adoring eyes when I told him what I thought of his paper."

"And you would have loved my forgiving him. Oh, heaven, Clark," she went on, clutching him. "What are we doing to each other?"

A man and a woman came out of Harry's Bar, their voices raised in disagreement.

"I just adored it," the woman was saying with a sigh. "That *fegato alla veneziana* was the best thing I ever tasted."

"At those prices, it should have been," the man replied grumpily. "Tasted like liver and onions to me."

"Oh, Martin, all you ever think about is money." The woman, plump and brassy, turned away in disgust.

"If you ever had to work to have it, you'd think twice about spending it, too." Martin struck a match, cupped his hand around the flame, and lit an enormous cigar.

Cringing inwardly, Maddy clutched Clark's arm. She had always been made miserable by the sight of a married couple at war. Of course all couples had their differences. She and Clark had more than once had it out, long before "beautifoil" came into their lives. But Martin and his wife were clearly doing more than fighting. Their essences were grating on each other. They were hating each other.

Were she and Clark dancing the first steps of a deadly waltz? Would a decade from now find them permanently crabbed and sour?

Every good marriage was a Venice, a light for all the world. And every bad marriage was a cloud. How many men and women started out shining with hope, only to end up like the couple who'd just come from Harry's Bar? She had always thought that she and Clark were set for life, immune to whatever infection it was that blighted love. Now suddenly she wasn't sure.

She felt hot and cold all at once. The air around her seemed unpleasantly damp.

"Hey," Clark said softly. "It's all right. We're not like that. You don't dye your hair. I don't smoke cigars."

"I wish we were having lunch on our own," she said. "What if you don't like Donatello?"

"Then I won't like Donatello." Clark shrugged his shoulders.

"But you'll still like me?"

"Yes, darling. Always and always."

They went inside.

Chapter 9

Lunch might have gone all right, Maddy thought later, if she and Clark had been alone with Donatello and Elena.

But Harry's Bar was hardly the place to get away from it all. The hub of Venetian social life since Ernest Hemingway's day, it drew everyone who was "in," Venetian or stranger, and everyone who longed to be.

The two couples from the Caffè alla Maddalena were there: Kitty and Lyle Dunn, the sleek dark-haired Justine Watters, and the man Maddy now knew to be a movie producer, Alex Emmerling. Ian Pargetter arrived soon after them, looking very happy to have escaped his tour group.

By the time the meal had progressed to fruit and cheese—a tangy, slightly waxy, yet sweet Tallegio—all the people Maddy knew were sitting together. The talk was of Maddy and the contest. Pargetter said she should write a book, with his help. Emmerling liked the idea of a movie. And Donatello was already mentally designing the wall fabric for the first American Donatello boutique.

Maddy's head swam. She held onto Clark's hand. She kept bringing him into the conversation. "Who will play Clark in the movie? What we need is a young William Powell. If there's a boutique, the decor should center around fresh flowers. Donatello, Clark does with flowers what you do with fabric. He'll put together a dozen different yellow flowers, so you realize for the first time how many yellows there are in the world."

There were several polite nods.

These people were missing the point about Clark. She felt she should be angry at them. Yet for some reason she was angry at Clark.

What had Donatello teasingly called her earlier? An inverse snob. That's what Clark was. If these were ordinary, anonymous people, he would give them the benefit of every doubt. If they were dull, he would find kindness in them. If they were shrill, he would say that life had never taught them softness. He would, in any event, go out to them, not sit there toying with his food, waiting for the others to prove themselves to him.

Margery Cahn, a stunning, dark-haired California potter who had a house on the Lido, stopped by the overflowing table and invited everyone to a party that night. Maddy remembered reading about her parties in one of those slick magazines she looked at for ten minutes every month while waiting to have her hair cut. She looked eagerly at Clark. He grimly nodded his head.

At the end of the meal Donatello said to Maddy, "Do not worry about what to wear tonight. I will have something delivered to the Gritti Palace by six. And a tie for you," he said to Clark. "You do sometimes wear a tie?"

"You do sometimes wear a tie?" Clark mimicked savagely, as he and Maddy walked away from the restaurant. "It's not as if I were the only man at Harry's Bar in an open-necked shirt. I suppose you'd like to see me in a double-breasted suit with a nipped-in waist."

"What if I did want to see that?" Maddy asked softly. "Just for a change. Would that be such an insult?" Then, unable to bear their bickering another moment, she said impulsively, "Clark, take me to your Venice."

"My Venice?"

"I bet you found something marvelous on your walk this morning. Share it with me. Can't we just be two tourists for a few hours, anonymous except to each other? Let's go to Murano and look at the awful glass. Do all the corny things."

"You mean it?"

His voice was so eager that she ached for him; what a miserable time he must be having that a change of pace was so welcome.

"I mean it. I need it as much as you do. And you know what else I need? To go back to our room and change."

"I've gotten used to the dress," Clark said. "It really does suit you."

"It's not the dress so much, it's the shoes. I need to change into flat sandals."

Companionably silent, they walked past the church of San Moise and down the crowded, cosmopolitan Calle Large XXII Marzo. Clark, the history buff, said it had been named after the 1848 revolution against the Austrians.

"We should have a July Fourth Street in Honeydale," Maddy declared. "That would be a good contest, wouldn't it? To think up the best new street name?" The reference to contests slipped out before she could stop it, but Clark seemed to understand its innocence. He squeezed her hand.

Looking in a shop window, Maddy saw something that made her gasp. Buttery-soft shoulder bags and handbags in sherbet-color leathers were all adorned with small square contrasting leather monograms reading JL.

"Jill Laverty!" she exclaimed.

Clark pointed to the sign over the entrance. "Jacobello Lombardo."

They went into the shop, and Maddy chose a mammoth raspberry carryall for her never-quite-organized friend, then added a monogrammed wallet and cosmetics case. She would have bought more, but Clark convinced her that Jill would only be embarrassed.

Maddy suddenly missed the warm, great-hearted Jill. She thought guiltily of how Donatello and Elena had dismissed her, based on a photograph. If she, Maddy, were an average five feet six, like Jill, instead of a striking five feet ten; if she were slightly overweight instead of decidedly thin; if she had freckles and ordinary lashes and a vague chin: Would her Venetian crowd be her crowd? She had always enjoyed her looks, but she'd never depended on them.

To ward off the confusing questions buzzing in her brain, she held Clark's hand tightly all the way back to the hotel. But one question wouldn't go away. When she got home to Honeydale, would she maybe find Jill a little boring?

"Let's call the Lavertys when we get up to the room," she said as they arrived back at the velvet welcome of the Gritti Palace.

"Anything special?" Clark asked.

"I just want to know if Honeydale is still there."

It was Saturday, and, with their kids at camp, the Lavertys were having breakfast when the operator reached them.

"Maple-flavored French toast," Jill said with a laugh over the hollow-sounding wire. "Doesn't need any syrup. I'm going to enter it in the Spring Run Bake-Off. Are there any towns with canals in Vermont?"

"No, but we haven't seen much in the way of mountains here," Maddy retorted. "What's new?"

"Let's see. The woodchucks are eating our garden. They're having double coupons next week at the Econo-Shop. Con wants to go to a movie tonight, and I want to play Bingo at the church. What do you mean, what's new? We're in Honeydale. What's new with you?"

"It's really beautiful, and we've met some interesting people," Maddy said vaguely. She was thinking that maybe the call hadn't been such a good idea. "We've been in a gondola, and we ate at Harry's Bar, and St. Mark's Basilica is the most amazing building I've ever seen."

There was a crackle, and Maddy thought the line was dead. Then Jill came back as clear as if she were next door. "Have you met Donatello?"

"This morning. I really like his clothes."

"Of course you like his clothes," Jill said, with a little groan. "Everyone but you knew you would like his clothes."

"I bought you something marvelous," Maddy blurted out. She fingered an appealing imperfection in the heavy raw silk bedspread.

"An ashtray from Murano?"

"Something better," Maddy said. "But I'll get you an ashtray if you want one."

"Maddy, this is a no-smoking household, remember?"

"Of course I remember. But for parties." Quickly, she went on,

"Would you call Clark's mother and send our love? I'm afraid it would be too exciting for her if we called. She belongs to the generation that takes long-distance calls to mean disaster."

"As soon as we hang up," Jill promised. "I'm sure she's fine."

"You haven't heard anything from Ramatak?" Maddy's voice trembled, though of course she knew the answer. The twins' camp had instructions to call the Lavertys in an emergency, and had there been an emergency, Jill and Con would have called Venice.

"Not a word. I'm sure the girls are great. They'll probably refuse to come home at the end of July."

Maddy knew the words were meant to be comforting, but her throat suddenly ached with unshed tears. Though the last thing she wanted was for Nellie and Kendra to be homesick, the next to last thing she wanted was for them not to miss her at all.

Oh, Lord, did they resent her for winning the contest the way Clark—and now Jill—seemed to?

"You keep having a great time," the voice from America said. "I've got to hang up and go do my laundry. Love to Clark."

"Mine to Con," Maddy said dully, then put the receiver down.

Silently she took off her dress. Her slip was clinging to her body and felt clammy. She would take a two-minute shower, she told Clark, then put on something cotton.

"Why so glum, puss-cat?" he asked gently.

"I don't think Jill was very glad to hear from me."

Clark sat down next to her on the bed. "Maybe an overseas phone call at daytime rates was kind of rubbing her face in it. For ten years the Lavertys have sent us postcards when they've gone on vacation, and we've done the same. She's probably afraid of losing you. I know the feeling."

With a mental apology to the maid who'd put the bed together so neatly, Maddy sneaked a pillow out from under the spread, then stretched out. "You were both happier for me than I was in the beginning." She gave a great sigh. "It's not as if I'm running away from you to some other world. Wherever I go, I want to take you with me. Should we send for the Lavertys?"

"Come on, Maddy."

"Well, why not?" she burst out. "It's not as if I earned the money by the sweat of my brow. It was luck. This is money to be shared."

"It was more than luck," Clark said. His fingers made soothing motions in her hair. "It wasn't just a sweepstakes, you know."

"If it wasn't luck, Jill deserves some of the credit. For being in that photograph." Even as she was speaking, she was thinking that she couldn't visualize Jill and Con at Harry's Bar. At least not with the "in" crowd.

Hating herself for her thoughts, she buried her face in the pillow. Everyone's worst suspicions were confirmed. Her values were changing. The loyalty that Elena Maggiore had praised her for the day before was a sham.

"I don't think you're going to see much of my Venice that way," Clark said gently.

Turning to meet his eyes, she was struck by the tenderness there. "Make love to me," she said softly. "Not the way we did last night, but wide awake. With that wondrous light streaming in the windows."

He traced an S-curve under her chin and down her throat. Bending over her, he brushed a silken kiss across her mouth. His hands as tender as if he were handling a baby, he peeled off her slip. "Mmm, salty," he said, as he lazily licked the shallow crevice between her perky breasts.

"I'll go take a shower," she said, starting to get up.

He pushed her back onto the bed. "You're just going to need another shower after what I do to you. Besides, I like the taste. It's the sea. The *scirocco* must be blowing."

"Someone else said that. Isn't that one of those winds that makes people go crazy?"

"It is." Clark's tongue flicked at her left nipple until it sang, then, in the interests of justice, flicked at the right.

As his mouth traveled down the faint line child-bearing had left on her belly, Maddy felt her thoughts recede. Pure sensations crowded her brain, a swirl of light and color.

"Clark," she called out faintly. The need to say his name grew more urgent. "Clark. Darling. Clark."

His tongue circled her navel, then dived in. The sensation unnerved her first, but the desire to giggle quickly turned into plain passion.

When he got to her wispy bikini panties, his mouth kept on going. As if the apricot silk were her skin, he licked and gently nipped, causing earth tremors in the flesh below.

"I want you," Maddy moaned. The sound of her own desire inflamed her further.

Clark's only answer was to run his tongue up and down her thighs, one, then the other, back and forth so quickly that all of her felt touched at once. As he snaked around to the backs of her knees, she thought she would explode.

Engulfing her toes one by one, he seemed to be making her love for him course down from her heart through all the channels of her body.

"Please," she heard herself say again and again, not knowing what she was begging for, knowing only that she had to utter the word.

He broke away from her, but only for seconds, to strip off his clothes and dispense with her panties. She saw that the acts he had performed on her body had aroused no less desire in his own. Her soul leaped at the knowledge that pleasing her pleased him so. Then they were fused in ecstatic union. Mouths clamped together, eyes open, they were bonded everywhere.

As they came back from that world to this, Clark said, "That's what I call my Venice."

Maddy snuggled into the delicious thereness of his arms. "If the rest of the tour is half as good, sign me on."

An hour later, he was saying, "Well? Is it half as good?"

They were on the far side of the Rialto Bridge, in the midst of the largest, most variegated, brightest-hued fruit and vegetable market Maddy had ever seen. Veronese and the other master artists of Venice might have designed it, so forcefully did it hit the eye.

"And I thought peppers were only peppers," she said, gaping in front of a stall heaped high with bursting globes in green, orange, and red. "I can't believe those colors."

"This is probably where Donatello gets his inspiration," Clark said.

Maddy poked him playfully. "I didn't bring up the name. You did." She looked at women, ranging from flashing-eyed teens to *nonnas* garbed in black, pinching and sniffing the gorgeous produce before stuffing it into string bags. "I wonder if it makes your life different to shop like this instead of buying old, pale veggies in plastic packages at the Econo-Shop."

"You never bought a pale plastic veggie in your life," Clark said. His arm slid companionably around her waist.

"No, but some women do," Maddy said seriously.

"Saves a lot of time," Clark said. "The women here aren't processing words, running for political office, or selling all-natural cosmetics."

"If Donatello designed potholders and aprons," Maddy mused, "maybe that would improve the quality of daily life for a lot of American women. Do you know how depressing a potholder can be?"

"You always scorch yours," Clark said with a knowing fondness. "That's why they look so awful." Guiding Maddy past mountains of oranges, grapes, and juicy figs, he said, "You're not going to let him talk you into opening a Donatello boutique in Honeydale, are you?"

"Is it such a bad idea?" Maddy returned. "I was thinking—there's the card shop that went out of business right near the greenhouse. That might be a perfect place. Unless you don't like the idea of having me so close every day." She stopped. "Oh, Clark. The perfume from those melons. I don't believe it."

"But he himself says he's never much appealed to American women. Nothing ever took off but his scarves."

"Because he wasn't designing for the American way of life. Now he's thinking differently."

"Look," Clark said, "I'm the last man on earth to underestimate the power of your impact—but, Maddy, something just doesn't ring true. If he's such a big deal, why does he need your help? And why did he get involved in the contest, by the way? He seems a little . . . hungry to me."

"You mean he's after our money?" Maddy asked, unable to keep the hurt from her voice.

"Well, who would capitalize this boutique?"

"Heaven, Clark, you're talking about an idea that didn't exist until this morning. Listen, the man lives in a *palace*. He probably doesn't even think of me as having money."

Suddenly Clark put his hands over Maddy's eyes. "Sniff," he said.

Inhaling, she caught whiffs of mint and an overlay of spice, mostly clove. It was a smell she knew almost as well as she knew the scent of her own home. "You've magically transported us to Whelan's Greenhouse, on a day when carnations have just arrived."

A kiss on the head told her she was right even before her eyes were uncovered. Her soul seemed to soar at the sight of so many carnations. She knew people who were indifferent to this common flower, some who actually disliked it, but she'd always been enchanted by its aroma. Besides, the ruffled petals always reminded her of the Kleenex carnations her mother had taught her to make—how well she remembered the time—when she was home from school with chicken pox.

She eyed some red-and-white-striped miniatures, evocative of Clark's favorite bathrobe. And there was an old favorite combination, miniatures that looked as though they'd been tie-dyed in yellow and orange.

"*Il fiore officiale di Venezia*," the vendor said with a smile. Wearing a peaked cap, his mouth missing several teeth, he was the classic vendor from a thousand postcards.

"The official flower of Venice," Maddy translated for Clark.

He reached for his wallet. "I can't believe I'm having to pay for flowers," he joked. As he pulled out *lira* notes, Maddy explained to the vendor that her husband also sold flowers.

Cradling the aromatic blooms, Maddy and Clark started across the Rialto Bridge. They paused to take in the panorama. Below on the Grand Canal, a gondola with a golden prow made its way toward the bridge, skimming lightly as a butterfly over the cerulean waves.

Suddenly the gondolier took off his straw hat and waved it. Impossible that he was waving at them, Maddy thought; then she realized it was Bondini. Impulsively she pulled a carnation from the bunch and sent it fluttering down toward the water. Bondini held out his hat and caught it.

Maddy and Clark applauded, as did the startled couple in the gondola.

"We can use you on the Yankees," Clark called down.

Clark's intent, if not his reference to the baseball team and Bondini's good catch, was apparently understood. The gondolier swept his hat in front of his waist and bowed.

Maddy glowed as Clark took her hand. That beautifully improbable moment with Bondini seemed like a blessing.

"Where to now?" she asked her husband.

"You'll see. At least, I hope you will," he added. "It's something I found this morning because I got lost. Let's see if I can lose us right again."

With her heart as light as it was, and in her flat sandals, Maddy felt as if she could walk forever. There was nothing in Venice that wasn't gorgeous to behold. Maybe the most beautiful sight, though the hardest to take, was a group of children playing with a soccer ball in a shadowed *campo*.

"Do you think we could invite them all for ice cream?" she asked wistfully.

Clark steered her decisively away. "What would you do if some Venetians visiting in Honeydale saw Nellie and Kendra playing and wanted to buy them ice cream?" he asked.

"I'd be suspicious, of course. I see your point."

They stopped for ice cream themselves. Maddy had *cremolatte* flecked with hazelnuts. Clark had chocolate. They stopped in a small shop and bought some marbled paper for Nellie and Kendra. Maddy had no idea what they would do with it, but she wanted them to have it.

She was fascinated by the way the weather seemed to change every time they turned a corner. In some of the big squares she felt the *scirocco* licking damply at her neck. Then they would pass through shadowy zones that made her wish for a sweater.

This was the ultimate all-and-everything city, all right. Was that why she and Clark had been struggling with themselves and each other? Because you couldn't have all-and-everything and not include some pain?

She felt she was on the verge of a new understanding that would make all the difference in her life. Words flew around in her mind but refused to coalesce into a thought. Before she left here she would have it. Bondini will tell me, she said to herself, then immediately felt foolish. It was enough that he'd caught that carnation! He didn't have to deliver up the secret of existence.

"I did it!" Clark was saying triumphantly. He pointed to an arrow on the wall and the word "Aquarium."

At first she felt disappointed. She was ready for a dose of great painting; she'd thought his mysterious destination was probably Accadémia.

But once inside she was ecstatic. The striped, spotted, and splatter-painted creatures swimming behind illuminated glass electrified her eyes. Never mind Titian and Tintoretto. Here was the signature of *the* master hand.

Alone in the small rectangular rooms, she and Clark wandered in awe, their arms around each other's waists.

"I think this is holier than St. Mark's," she whispered.

There was no mistaking his delight, his relief. "I knew you'd understand."

"How did you find it?" she asked. "Is it in the guide books?"

"I don't think so," Clark said. "I told you, I got lost. In Venice I think you have to get lost to get found."

His words echoed in her mind as she watched a chubby yellow and red creature chase a streamlined character done in a dozen shades of green.

"This is even better than the market," she said. "I'll bet Donatello comes here, too." She pointed to a blubbery-lipped creature swimming around a wavy plant. "I think I saw a shirt done in that peach-on-purple pattern."

A strange feeling grew in her stomach, so demanding of attention that she wished it would go away. It was desire, but more than desire. She wanted Clark to feel it, too, yet she was tempted to snatch her hand away so it wouldn't communicate itself, wouldn't become real.

"Are you okay, darling?" he asked.

"I think so." But she wasn't sure, and Clark saw her hesitation.

Concern etched on his face, he led her toward the exit. "I'm going to take you back to the hotel. It sounds as though we have quite an evening ahead on the Lido. We should probably take a nap." Playfully spanking her bottom, he added, "And that's not a euphemism, young woman, so don't get any ideas."

Chapter 10

THE SUN WAS SETTING BEHIND THEM as their *motoscafo* sped toward the Lido. Looking at the wild streaks of violet and salmon in the sky, Maddy thought that if colors had calories, she'd have gained fifty pounds today. She confided to Clark that she needed to rest her senses with a black-and-white movie.

Margery Cahn's house was almost as refreshing. Near the famed Excelsior Palace Hotel, and boasting its own precious strip of beach, it was decorated in white on white. The walls were hung with cool, hard paintings and prints that were vastly welcome to Maddy's eyes. A Josef Albers "Adobe" geometric in shades of gray was like a drink of pure mountain water, as was a William Horton pencil sketch of the snowy mountains of Gstaad.

But color ran riot in the laughing crowd that thronged the house. And no one was more colorful, Maddy knew, than she herself. The dress Donatello had left at the Gritti Palace was made up of hundreds of fluttering streamers over a lilac body slip, and no two streamers were the same. Some were solids, mainly in green tones. Others were swirling mixes of yellows and purples. One was bright with the earth tones of her hair.

It seemed entirely appropriate that, as they entered the vast living room, a trio was playing "Somewhere Over the Rainbow."

Kitty Dunn and Justine Watters were also wearing dreses by the young designer, though neither one was quite so flamboyant. But there was no sign of Donatello himself.

Maddy did and didn't feel part of the brilliant crowd. It seemed that everyone else knew everyone else. Kitty introduced her to a *principessa* and to a woman with pale frizzy hair to her waist who was apparently famous for her "performance art."

"We could cut up your dress," the young woman said, her solemn eyes wide, "and make the most beautiful confetti. Then we'll give you a parade and throw it over you."

Alex Emmerling came to drag Justine and Kitty away to the grilled shrimp.

"Or we could stand you in front of a fan," the performance artist said, "and let those streamers blow." Shivering, she added dramatically, "All those colors make me craaazy!"

Her companion, a wiry young man in denim, snatched a box of crayons out of his pocket. "I want to make you crazy!" he shouted. Extracting a red crayon, he feverishly began to draw a spiraling line down one of the sleeves of her billowy white cotton dress.

"I am red!" the young woman all but shrieked. She leaped into the air. "I am green," she groaned, rolling around on the floor as her companion dashed streaks of lime and pine down her back.

Maddy wasn't sure whether she was horrified, amused, or both. Clark said he was getting some great ideas for a game at Nellie's and Kendra's next party.

"Oh, God, the crayon piece again," Maddy heard a bored voice say behind her.

She turned to see the poignant features of Elzbieta Cezeska. After introducing the actress to Clark, she said, "You mean this isn't spontaneous?"

"Rehearsed to the teeth," Elzbieta said. "Not that they've succeeded in making it good."

Clark smiled in evident relief. "I was afraid I was going to get the

Clod of the Year award for not thinking it was wonderful. You mean I don't have to like it?"

The actress smiled encouragingly. "What kind of theater do you enjoy?"

"I'm not at all original," Clark said. "Give me Shakespeare anytime. I like passion, not tricks."

"This is a good man," Elzbieta declared to Maddy. "Hold on to him. Uh-oh," she added quickly, "here comes one of the world's ten great bores. Time for me to go swimming. He's afraid of the water." She made a hasty exit through dramatic French doors.

"Swimming!" Maddy exclaimed to Clark. "What a perfect night for it. I wish we'd thought to bring suits."

Clark gestured around at the merry crowd. "What makes you think this gang bothers with suits? These are the swingers of the world, my darling. Nothing so middle class as suits for them."

Maddy watched a blonde in black and pearls squeal with delight as a balding man dropped an ice cube into her gaping décolletage, then retrieved it.

"Maybe you're right," she said to Clark.

"I am sun, I am moon, I am lemons. Warm yourself in me," cried the performance artist as she was scribbled on in yellow.

"I wonder where Donatello is," Maddy said.

"Changing the subject, darling? You mean you don't want to swim?"

She looked at him disbelievingly. "But the woman who owns this house is so nice," she began.

"Come on, now. We know nice people in Honeydale who like to skinny-dip."

"Oh, you mean the Ryders? Well, sure. In the privacy of their own pool." She looked at him for reassurance, "You never wanted to go to any of their parties, though."

Clark would not yield. "We were never invited."

A smiling waitress offered them a silver tray heaped with freshly steamed artichoke hearts.

Popping one into her mouth, Maddy all but swooned. "These have no relation at all to those artichoke hearts in bottles," she said. "They're fantastic." Looking up at Clark, batting her eyelashes, she feigned regret. "Oh, dear. Now I can't go swimming for an hour."

Clark guided her to the French doors. "Look out there. Hardly any moon. You drop your towel at the edge of the water, and no one sees a thing. Except for me."

Maddy stood there clutching him. "You really want that, don't you?" Behind them, the sounds of partying rose and fell.

"When I was a kid, we used to drive up to Vermont every summer, for the week of the Fourth of July." Clark's voice grew misty. "My mother would work her way through a yard of mystery books—I think that's where Nellie gets her love of Nancy Drew—and my father and I would go fishing. He had a favorite trout stream, and near it there was a natural waterfall and a swimming hole, and he'd take me there when he'd caught his limit. I'd pull off my clothes and jump in. I had the greatest sensation of freedom."

"I never knew about that." Maddy leaned her head against his shoulder. "Still learning about you after all these years."

"Should I be the only one learning?" He couldn't keep a touch of acid out of his voice. "You talk about how complex everyone is, but sometimes I can't help thinking you'd like to do all the exploring while I stay the same. Oh, you'd like me to get a white suit, maybe, and make brittle conversation with brittle people—but I wonder how much you'd like even those changes if they happened."

Maddy's cheeks grew hot. "All right, I'll go swimming with you."

"No, not if you're going to be miserable about it."

"I'm not miserable," Maddy said, "but give me a minute to get used to the idea. I wouldn't let Donatello look at me in a slip today."

"Of course not." Clark encircled her shoulders. "Your husband wasn't there to protect you."

After a minute Maddy said, "They're not all brittle people, are they? Didn't you like Elzbieta?"

"Yes, and I like our hostess." Gesturing toward an unglazed cylindrical vase full of carnations, he added, "And I like her pots."

"What about Donatello?" Maddy persisted. "He may not be a

down-home good ol' buddy like Con, but you have to admit he's talented. And I think he's basically nice."

Clark sighed. "I don't know, honey. I want to like him, I really do, but he doesn't ring true for me. Something's going on there that makes me wary. I hope you'll think twice about any involvement." He gave a little laugh. "Hey, this is a party. We're supposed to have fun. Let's dance."

He didn't have to ask twice. Not only did she love any excuse to be in his arms, but also Margery Cahn's musicians were playing their kind of music—show tunes from the thirties, forties, and fifties. Love may have been no more reasonable then, but at least it had rhythm and rhyme.

"I bet you expected wild disco stuff," she twitted to Clark as they moved easily to the strains of "Once You Find Your Guy."

"I didn't dare think about the music," Clark said, holding her tight.

Leaning against his broad shoulder, she felt more peaceful than she had since landing at Marco Polo Airport three days earlier. There remained the question of the nude swim, but she knew Clark wouldn't push her. He'd never pushed her about anything.

After their dance they refreshed themselves with a fruity young white wine from Collio Goriziano, near the Yugoslavian border. They chatted with an Irish diplomatic couple and with a former professional football player from Minnesota who was going to run for Congress.

"You see?" Maddy teased Clark. "You're not the only ex-football player here. Doesn't that make you feel better?"

He did seem to be having a genuinely good time, she thought, even asking Justine Watters to dance when Alex Emmerling asked Maddy. What was making tonight different from their thornier hours in Venice?

Of course! No one was discussing the contest. They weren't Madeline-Whelan-who-won-half-a-million and what's-his-name.

But when Ian Pargetter arrived at the party, Clark tensed up again. The Australian publishing baron made a beeline for the Whelans.

"How well do you know Donatello?" he asked without preamble.

"Better than I'd like to," Clark said grimly. He amended his words a moment later. "Not at all well. We just met him today."

Was it possible? Maddy felt as though she'd known the designer half her life. Maybe that illusion was fostered by wearing his clothes; she felt she'd seen the colors inside his mind.

"I've heard some disturbing rumors about him," Ian went on. "I'd like to track them down." He waggled his expressive gray eyebrows. "Could be a big story."

"You mean you've found out he comes from another planet?" Clark commented sarcastically.

The thin Australian roared with laughter. "You're never going to forgive me for that *Banner* story, are you? Shall I have the reporter fired?"

"No!" Maddy exclaimed.

"No," Clark agreed in a cooler voice. "Not unless you also punish the person who gave the hit order."

"Poor old Jimmy Willetz, who edits *The Banner*? Or were you thinking of me?" He suddenly clapped Clark on the back. "You're the real thing, as they say in the States, aren't you? A straight arrow. A man of honor."

For the first time since she'd known him, Maddy saw a patch of red on the broad planes of Clark's cheeks—whether from pleasure or anger or both, she didn't know.

"What's the scoop on Donatello?" Clark asked in a tone that was almost a growl, as though he was eager to discuss any life other than his own. Or maybe, Maddy thought, having made his point to Ian Pargetter, he could now afford to make peace.

"Gambling problems. Unpaid taxes. Italy takes taxes very seriously, you know."

As if on cue, Elzbieta Cezeska joined their little group. Her short blond hair, still wet from her swim, was slicked back. "Did Donatello say anything to you about when he was coming this evening? I've got another party back in Venice tonight, and he's invited too, I'd much rather make the crossing in his *motoscafo* than take the *vaporetto*."

Maddy said she thought he'd said something about seeing her around nine, but she wasn't sure.

Elzbieta's face looked troubled. "And he didn't offer any of us a ride across. That could mean trouble."

"What do you mean?" Maddy asked, concerned.

Elzbieta spread her delicate hands expressively. "You can't come to Margery's house without passing the casino."

"You mean Donatello is a compulsive gambler?" Ian Pargetter asked quickly.

Instantly Clark said to Elzbieta, "You should know that this is a newspaperman. Anything you say may appear in print. And things you don't say may also appear."

So he hadn't been interested in making peace, Maddy thought regretfully. But Ian Pargetter didn't look perturbed. No doubt he'd been assailed before, by less gentle tongues.

"I'm going to check the casino," Elzbieta said decisively.

"We'll go with you," Maddy said instantly.

Clark put a hand on her shoulder. "Darling, I know how loyal you are, even to the newest of friends, but this isn't your affair."

"I'm not so sure," Elzbieta said. "Maddy, do you remember this morning, how he called you his Lady Luck? He's stayed away from the tables for many months now, but maybe he saw your arrival as some kind of sign."

"Yes, I remember!" Maddy bit her lip. "And when he called me his Lady Luck, you and Elena exchanged nervous looks."

"What about Elena?" Clark put in. "Can't she keep him away from the gaming tables?"

"She is a strong, marvelous woman," Elzbieta said, "but she can do only so much. In the past she told him he had to choose between blackjack and her, and he chose her, thank God. But tonight . . ." She let the words hang.

"Let's go," Clark said.

As they trooped out of the house, Maddy heard Ian say to Clark, "You're a curious man, Whelan. At lunch this afternoon I had the feeling you had very little affection for Donatello. Yet you're quick to come to his defense. Eager to save him first from me, and now from himself." Jamming his hands into the pockets of his dinner jacket, the tall Australian added, "Why?"

"Because he's a man of honor," Maddy said, slipping her arm through Clark's.

"Now who's being corny?" Clark chided her, but he didn't sound displeased.

"He sacrificed himself for his father's—"

Clark put a gentle hand across her mouth. "Never mind about that. Please, Maddy."

"What do you do for a living?" Ian Pargetter asked.

"I'm a florist," Clark said shortly. "I don't suppose even you can make a headline out of that."

"Are you going to go on being a florist?" Ian persisted. "Or are you going to retire?" Rapidly calculating, he said, "After the government takes its bite, you've still got a quarter of a million. Which, properly invested, will bring you an effortless thirty thousand a year."

"We already knew that, thank you," Clark said. Then, as if tiring of his own brusqueness, he added, "We always planned to go back to college when we could afford to." He hesitated for a long moment, then added, "I assume that's still the plan."

"No Donatello boutique? No movie or book called *Pennies from Heaven*? And aren't you a little, shall we say, grown up to go back to college?"

"Don't you ever take a night off?" Clark asked, but not without amusement in his voice. "Don't you get tired of playing reporter?"

"Oh, it's all strictly off the record," Ian said. "And, no, I never stop being curious about my fellow man. And woman."

"A boutique wouldn't mean there couldn't be college," Maddy said. "Though we can't carve up *all* our time. We have eight-year-old twins. We're not about to let my winnings turn them into gold-plated latch-key kids. Besides—" Her voice faltered. "Well, just besides," she said, deciding she didn't care what everyone wondered.

They could hear music and laughter from the casino, and an indefinable excited murmur; Maddy decided it was the growling of a thousand bellies hungry for money. The brilliantly lit façade of the building was infinitely inviting. Its aura of glamour moved her for a moment. Then she thought of Donatello.

"Whelan," Ian Pargetter suddenly said, "I want you to work for me."

The Whelans and Elzbieta all stopped in their tracks. It seemed the least likely sentence to pass between the two men.

"I want to revamp *The Banner*. Hell, life is interesting enough without making stories up. I was lazy about *The Banner*. Bought it a year ago and just let it keep going its merry way. But why? Who needs it? And, frankly, it isn't even making much money. I think people would pay more for truth." Picking up a small pebble and throwing it with the merry abandon of a boy, he said, "Be my publisher. Turn *The Banner* into a paper you'd be proud to have your kids read. A paper of honor."

Maddy realized she was holding her breath. She clutched Clark's hand.

"I don't know the first thing about publishing," Clark said quietly.

"You know how to run a business, don't you? You're a fast learner, I can see that. And, above all, you know about honor." Laughing disarmingly, he added, "Probably better than I do. Of course, you wouldn't be able to go back to college. But I guarantee you that the newspaper business is the best education a man can have. It even takes you to Venice to see the basilica portal mosaics and to defend innocent women's behinds." He clapped Clark on the shoulder. "Don't answer me now. It's one to sleep on. But, for heaven's sake, don't wake up in the morning thinking it was a joke."

Holding Clark's hand, Maddy could feel the tremors of excitement going through both of them. What an extraordinary turn of events! Only in Venice! Was he considering saying yes, or had he already dismissed the idea? They hadn't yet made concrete plans about college; first one of them, then the other, had suggested postponing all plan-making until after the Venice trip. And then there was the aquarium— but why was she thinking about the aquarium? Reliving that strange desire in her belly? She felt doors trying to close in her mind, against a wind trying to blow them open. The *scirocco*? She did feel damp.

If there was any place on earth where her dress of brilliant streamers could feel run-of-the-mill, it was at the casino. And if there was ever a time when Maddy was glad to be distracted, it was now. She saw shimmering hand-beaded dresses; yards of diamonds, emeralds, pearls against lustrous tanned skin; and white summer furs worth many thousands of dollars worn as casually as last year's sweater. The men, though less splashy, were uniformly splendid, their tailoring and air of power worthy of James Bond.

But when she saw Donatello, the glitter looked like so much tinsel. Pale, sweating, glassy-eyed, he sat at the blackjack table. Elena, stunning in red and silver but her dynamism stilled, stood behind him.

"Lady Luck!" Donatello cried hoarsely as Maddy approached. He watched stricken as the dealer raked chips across the green felt-covered table. "You will turn it all round for me."

Elzbieta looked at Elena. "Bad?"

Elena fought to keep control. "Everything he had saved to pay the first installment on his tax bill. The government won't give him another chance." Turning savagely on Maddy, she raged, "Why did you have to come with your crazy American dreams?"

"Now, wait a minute—" Clark began strongly, but Elena had started to weep.

"I am sorry, signora. Forgive me. It is not your fault that contest inflamed him. Such a beautiful, absurd notion, five hundred thousand dollars for some silly words—excuse me, signora—about the stuff you wrap leftovers in."

The dealer, expressionless behind his visor, was expelling cards rapid-fire from a shoe. Donatello had an ace showing, the dealer a seven. Peeking at his hole card, Donatello tapped a chip against the table to let the dealer know he wanted another card. And another. And one more made eighteen showing; with the hole card he had twenty. But the dealer didn't bust, as the players and kibitzers had hoped; he had twenty-one.

"Come with us," Maddy urged Donatello. "You're missing a fabulous party."

"But I cannot go, Lady Luck." Indicating his pathetic pile of chips, he said, "With your help I can still turn it around."

"Yes, you can," Maddy said fiercely, "but not here. If you want your American boutique, you have to come away now."

Donatello looked close to tears. "I thought to have enough to pay my tax bill and finance the boutique," he said. "Oh, the dreams I have dreamed today!"

"Your dreams can still come true," she said to him, "but not here. You will only find nightmares here."

The others at the table went on with their play. A dowager

whose blue-rinsed hair was studded with sapphires said softly, "It's a shame." Maddy wondered whether she was talking about Donatello's plight, or scolding Maddy and the others for intruding on her pleasure.

"Come on, Donatello," Ian Pargetter said crisply. "I've got a proposition for you. But I refuse to discuss it here."

Donatello looked at the table, at his fellow players, at the dealer. He looked at the marble-faced Elena, at the pleading faces of his friends. From the nightclub came sudden music, the sound of an orchestra striking up "Luck, Be a Lady Tonight."

His brown eyes glittered as they fixed on Maddy's. Not daring to speak, she nodded encouragingly.

Donatello scraped back his chair and rose to his feet. With a gesture Maddy found oddly touching, he pushed his remaining chips toward the dealer: a tip.

Maddy held her breath until their group was safely outside the pleasure palace. Elena could not hold back a sob. Donatello threw an arm around her.

"We'll be all right, *cara mia*," he said, his jaunty swagger returning.

"But how? The government will take it all. The palace, the fabrics . . ."

"I'd like to offer you a commission," Ian Pargetter said, as casual as anything. "I'd like the Big Kangaroo redecorated."

"The big kangaroo?" Donatello asked, not comprehending.

Ian made hopping motions that brought a smile to every face. "My private plane," he said. "It's looking a little shabby. I don't know much about fabrics, but I know I like yours. I suppose it'll cost me a fortune to hire you," he mused. "Probably—what's the size of your tax bill?"

Mumbling, Donatello revealed the figure.

"I'll pay the bill directly," Ian said. "We'll work out the rest of the details. Assuming, of course, that you want the commission."

"I'll have to think about it," Donatello began airily, then burst out laughing as Elena gave him an unsubtle kick. "Yes, that sounds very interesting, Signore Pargetter. Tell me, what made you decide to redo your plane—besides an appreciation for my genius? I must understand you, you see, if I am to do the job right."

105

Ian gazed out toward the Adriatic, at waves kissed with moonlight. "I thought I came to Venice to do a simple reporting job and maybe expose a kind of crook—a man who doesn't give people their money's worth. Then someone forced me to see that maybe I have been that same sort of crook. I'm a very rich man," he added simply. "I don't have to exploit. I can afford to live by the highest standards. I think I want to redecorate the plane to remind me, wherever I go, of the lights of Venice. And the brightest light is truth, isn't it?" Smiling, he added, "Am I making any sense?"

"You are to me," Elzbieta Cezeska said, making Maddy wonder about the twists and turns in the actress's life. Someday, she hoped, they would know each other better. With a little start she realized that the glamorous Polish woman reminded her of Jill. Jill would have gone over to the casino on a rescue mission, the same way Elzbieta had done.

When they got back to Margery Cahn's house, Maddy hung back from the others. Clark looked inquiringly at her.

"I need to cool off after all that's happened," she said. "I need to go for a walk on the beach. Actually, I need to swim."

Hand in hand, they walked across a wide patio. At the foot of it, where the stone gave way to sand, there was a divided cabana. Going into the women's side, Maddy took off her dress, panty stockings, and sandals. She wrapped a huge pink towel around herself, looked into the mirror, and shrugged.

Venice! Would the wonders never cease?

Stepping outside the cabana, she caught her breath. Clark was waiting for her, a towel around his waist: Clark, and the sea, and the night. No other partygoers were on the beach now. It was as if they all understood that Clark and Maddy deserved this moment alone.

They walked silently to the edge of the water. The gentle lapping souud filled Maddy's ears. A buoy bell clanged, then stopped. She heard one lone cry from some creature of the sea.

She dropped her towel. The warm breath of the *scirocco* embraced her, teasing her; it tongued every inch of her surface and found the secret parts.

Then Clark was naked, too. She stared in awe. She'd never before seen him naked outdoors. What she felt was more and less than desire. She wanted him, yes, but not just for himself; she wanted him because he was part of the whole great, gorgeous scheme of things. The aquarium flashed into her mind again. She'd felt that desire there. And something else: a kind of demand that was being made on her—but what? And from where?

Lust and purity all at once. That intoxicating freedom Clark had recalled from his boyhood summers.

And more.

Religion? Some mystical sensation that the universe stood revealed? Not chaos, but ultimate sense?

Yes. And more.

"Maddy?"

"Hi."

"Do you want to tell me what's bothering you?"

"I would if I knew." She gave him her hand. "Honest," she said to his searching glance. Then: "Let's go swimming. Come on."

The water was a shock at first, a crazy kind of high. She took the plunge and got wet all over. "Whee!" she shouted, and felt better. She was suddenly a primitive spirit; she had always lived in the water.

Clark picked her up and twirled her around. He put her on his shoulders and ran.

"Giddap, fishie!" she cried. She felt all of fourteen years old, except that her nipples were incredibly hard.

They kissed, blue lips against blue lips, chattering teeth against chattering teeth. They raced back to the cabana.

Daring, Clark came over to the "Signora" side. Taking a dry towel, he briskly rubbed Maddy everywhere.

"Love you, love you, love you," he murmured. The towel lingered between her legs.

She licked the salt taste from his lips. "Was it as good? Venice with me as Vermont without me?"

"Everything's better with you."

She pulled her dress over her head. "Let's go look at paintings tomorrow. Do you realize how many paintings we haven't seen? And I want to go to the basilica."

"You mean it's been a disappointing day?" He buttoned his white shirt.

"Yup. Not a single thing happened I can put on a postcard. If I write about the aquarium, everyone will think we're really at Coney Island."

She shivered, and not just from the cold; Clark's arms were deliciously welcome.

"Maddy, if I took the job that Ian Pargetter offered, you could still go to college. There are plenty of schools within easy driving distance. If you arranged your schedule right, you could be home in time to meet the school bus."

She broke out of his embrace to look at him. "I don't know," she began.

"Look, I know that college was something we were going to do together, but—"

"I understand." She pulled up her panty stockings. She fastened her sandals.

"You don't look as though you understand." Pulling on his navy blazer, Clark added, "I know this wasn't the most brilliant time to bring up the future. But obviously it's been on both our minds. He did mean it, Maddy?"

"Of course he meant it." The damp smell of the cabana was suddenly oppressive. "I suppose you would travel a lot."

"Some, maybe. I'm not sure. I think the publisher sends other people places. Or is that the editor's job?"

"Let's go back to the party," Maddy said abruptly.

"What's the matter, darling?" Clark asked as they clicked across the patio. "I could have sworn you were almost jumping out of your skin when he made his offer."

"And you'd still want me to go back to college?" she pressed.

"Why not? Unless . . ."

"Unless what?" she probed.

"Well, the boutique," he said lamely. "I suppose you have notions now about rescuing Donatello."

"Well, if he and Elena moved to the States, he'd be eligible to enter all sorts of sweepstakes. I'd get him a subscription to the *Contest News-*

Letter. Maybe that would fulfill the gambling urge, without getting him into trouble."

Clark laughed fondly. "Oh, Maddy Whelan, you're one in a million."

"I know it's awfully naïve, and I suppose he needs professional help, but still—" She broke off abruptly. "Clark, I'm not sure I do want to go back to college. Not because of Donatello or a boutique, but—well, dreams change. You've found something maybe more important to do, and that leaves me—"

He squeezed her hand. "I understand."

"Do you?"

He said again that he did. But she thought that really he couldn't because she didn't understand herself. If they went back to the aquarium together, maybe . . .

Her mind was full of mists now. She welcomed the music and lights and voices—the obliterating laughs—of the party.

"Drink me, I'm wine!" the performance artist cried as her friend empurpled her with crayon.

Maddy joined the circle around her, clapping and cheering her on.

Chapter 11

I'm NOT TAKING PARGETTER UP ON HIS OFFER," Clark said the next morning.

They were sitting outside Quadri, on the Piazza San Marco, catching the morning sun, eating crusty rolls, and drinking strong coffee.

"You're not?" Maddy tried to keep her voice neutral. This was Clark's decision.

"Well, I'd really hate to have to start paying for all our flowers."

The joke fell flat.

"You don't really trust him?" Maddy suggested.

"No, I really do. Maybe I'm being naïve, but I can't see why a man of his stature would make a phony offer. I'm sure he'll also bail out Donatello. I think when he wants to destroy, he goes after bigger game. Like that multimillion-dollar tour business he wants to expose."

Maddy sipped her coffee. One thing had surely changed forever in her life, and that was her feeling about this particular beverage. She intended to bring home an espresso machine.

"Why turn him down, then?" she asked.

Clark's gray eyes were sober. "We don't want to forget all the old dreams, do we? I think we'd be making a mistake to jettison the idea of college." Striving for a smile, he added, "I can just see all four of us gathered around in the evening, doing our homework. Fun."

Maddy nodded. "Yes, it would be." But she closed her eyes as she spoke; the picture looked somehow wrong.

"I could keep the greenhouse going, though I'd bring in a manager. If the Donatello business takes off, we can spend a lot of our vacations in Venice. Then after college, who knows? Maybe I'll look up Parget-ter again. I have to admit he turned my head a bit. I'd like to go public with my ideals."

"When are you going to tell Ian?" she asked.

"I thought I'd walk over to the Bauer Grünwald now. Then you and I can meet and go look at all those paintings you wanted to catch up with."

"All right." Impulsively she added, "Can we meet at the aquarium?"

"If you're sure you can find it again."

"I'm sure."

He hesitated. "Do you want to come with me?"

"No, I think this is something you'd rather do on your own." She gave a little laugh. "With you and Ian together, who's going to protect my virtue?"

"I have to admit you look very luscious," Clark said, smiling at her simple cotton dress and pearls. "I'm not sure Donatello would approve of that pale blue and white, but I certainly do."

"Jill picked it out just before we left," Maddy said. She made a wry face. "She may have different ideas from Donatello, but she's the one who should run a boutique if anyone should. She loves clothes. I think she'd rather run a shop than go on being a substitute teacher. She was talking about burnout last spring. And her working days were too few and far between."

"Well, can't she be part of the grand scheme?" Clark asked.

Maddy broke off a bit of bread and boldly dunked it in her coffee. "I just don't think it would be great chemistry. Donatello and Elena saw her picture, and, well, they were kind of disparaging." Making a face, she added, "I didn't think we would still be friends after that."

"What picture?" Clark asked.

"You know. The one we took for the contest."

"Did Jill ever sign a release?" he asked. "I can't believe they could send copies of that picture around without her permission. What do you bet they shot a similar scene, using a model?"

Maddy's face lit up. "Oh, I hope you're right. That's been sticking in the way of my happiness. You know how I want the people I care for to care for each other."

"Which means you want the whole world to embrace." Clark's smile was affectionate and proud. "Has there ever been anyone, darling, you didn't end up liking?"

"There was that nasty bus driver."

The two of them laughed at the memory of that long-ago unpleasantness. In New York City with the twins, on their way to the Museum of Natural History, Maddy had suddenly discovered she didn't have the right change. The driver had yelled about "out-of-towners and their brats." But, upset as she'd been, especially for the children, Maddy had brushed off Clark's suggestion that she report him. He was obviously a man with troubles aplenty, she had said. She wasn't going to make his life worse.

"Maddy, about the job with *The Banner*."

"Yes?" she said eagerly.

"I suppose the money would be terrific. Would you like that part of it, darling? After our taste of traveling luxury class?"

Maddy looked out at the piazza. "I think it's nice to have enough money so you don't have to think about money. But we've got that." Covering his hand, she said, "In a way, we always had it."

"Let's be realistic," he said. "After the house for my mother, and enough set aside to educate the kids and maybe get the boutique going—"

"We'll have enough," Maddy said quietly. "The boutique will make lots of money. Especially if Jill comes in with me. Even if I—" She swallowed. "Even if I spend most of my time at college. Money is definitely not the reason to take that job."

She sat on at the table after Clark had left, trying to sort out her thoughts. She was almost there, she thought, on the verge of making terrific sense. But she needed a push over the edge.

Suddenly she had an idea. Bondini! It was Sunday, and maybe she shouldn't bother him—but, no, he had made it quite clear. She was to ask the manager at the Gritti Palace to find him when she needed him. Whatever the day or time.

The man in charge of the front desk at the hotel seemed not to have heard of Bondini. He offered to find her another gondolier, the most knowledgeable about Venice, with the most comfortable and elegant boat.

No, it had to be Bondini, she said. He'd collected them at the hotel's private landing before. A tall man, thin, with gray hair.

The man behind the desk spread his hands.

His assistant paused in the act of checking through a pile of passports. "Bondini. *Sì*. Domenico Bondini."

Maddy smiled. The word for Sunday in Italian was *domenica*. Surely Domenico Bondini would be found for her today.

The assistant thumbed through a small, dog-eared telephone book, its shabbiness conspicuous in this ancient bower of elegance. "No telephone," he muttered. "But there's a *caffè* downstairs." Dialing a number, he spoke in what Maddy now knew to be the Venetian dialect. He paused—while someone ran upstairs for Bondini?—then spoke again. Looking at Maddy, he asked, "You are the American signora he took out the day before yesterday?"

Maddy smiled. "I am."

"He will be at the landing in fifteen minutes."

As Bondini helped her into his golden-prowed craft, Maddy knew a moment of fear. Whatever he showed her today would be truth from which she could not turn away. Was she ready for that moment of recognition?

She had no choice, she decided. She owed it to herself, to Clark, to their children, in some way to all the world, to follow her instinct.

Bondini was smiling at her. "*Buon giorno*, Signora Maddalena."

A shiver spiraled up her spine. So she hadn't been mistaken. He was a man who knew things he couldn't know.

"*Buon giorno*, Signore Bondini," she replied. She fumbled for the words that would tell him he was kind to come out on a Sunday.

"*Piacere*, signora," he said graciously, as if he could imagine no greater pleasure.

"I have to be at the aquarium at noon," she told him. "But meanwhile I'd like to see . . ." She hesitated. "What you want me to see. The most important sight in Venice."

He nodded vigorously, wielding his long steering pole. "That is easy, signora," he said. "You have seen the Ducal Palace, Accadémia, the Rialto?"

"Yes," she said, "but I didn't mean—"

Bondini laughed gently. "I know you didn't, signora. Trust me. Lean back and relax and enjoy the view. I will take you to see what you want to see. The most important sight in Venice."

To Maddy's surprise, he didn't head into the Grand Canal but turned and started for wider water.

"You are taking me to Murano?" she asked doubtfully.

"No, signora. This is not the way to Murano. And Murano does not contain the ultimate treasure. I am taking you to Giudecca."

"Ah. The Church of the Redentore," she guessed. Her guide book had proclaimed it Palladio's "masterwork" and said it wasn't to be missed. Next Sunday, the third in July, there would be the gala Festa del Redentore. A bridge of boats would be built connecting Giudecca with the Venetian mainland. There would be fireworks, singing, dancing.

"The Redentore is beautiful, signora," Bondini said, "but that is not our destination."

"The Church of Sant' Eufemia? Le Zitelle?" she guessed. She knew she was babbling nervously, but she couldn't help herself.

"You will see what you will see," Bondini said. "Have patience. We are almost there."

The waters were crowded with other boats as they grew near the slim island. Fishing boats at rest for the day. She felt guilty again about having summoned Bondini on a Sunday. He probably had a family. And he certainly needed a day of rest.

Passing the Church of the Redentore, Bondini guided the gondola into a canal. Drawing abreast of some shadowy steps, he said, "We are here." He threw a rope around a pole and began to make the boat fast.

Maddy suddenly felt very nervous. What did she know about this man? Clark had more than once called her too quick to trust—the sort of person who never had learned that you don't take candy from strangers. She had expected Bondini to drop her off somewhere, she realized, not get out of the boat with her. Had she invited him to think she wanted—? She stifled the unpleasant thought.

Oh, well. The man at the hotel knew Bondini had collected her at the landing. So when she didn't show up at the aquarium and Clark sounded the alarm . . .

"Don't be afraid, signora," Bondini was saying. His weathered face was creased with silent laughter.

She told herself she was being foolish. Dear Best-Buy Corporation, she wrote on a postcard in her mind. Having wonderful time. Wish you were here. Today I saw a part of Venice they don't talk about in the guide books. It was beautiful beyond my wildest dreams.

From the steps Bondini led her across a square where light and shadow played games with each other. Here were simple signs of commerce—a shoe-repair shop, a pharmacy—that reminded her of something, but she couldn't remember what. Then her brain took a jog, and she realized: Honeydale. Three blocks from the quiet street where the Whelans lived there was a small zone of service shops—Clem's Cwik Cleaners, a pharmacy, a tobacco shop; and an old-fashioned ice cream shop just about where the *caffè* was that Bondini was leading her to.

But he wasn't taking her into the caffè, from which a tantalizing smell of espresso emanated. He was holding open a door and inviting her into a dark hallway.

She hesitated, not wanting to give offense, not wanting to take a foolish chance.

"Signora, sometimes you must go where it is darkest to see the light." But still she hesitated, and he laughed and called up the stairs, "Maria!"

Maddy heard the clattering of young feet on the stairs. A bright-eyed girl of about sixteen, lustrous dark hair flowing to her shoulders, appeared.

"*Sì*, Papa?" she said, looking at Bondini adoringly.

"This is Signora Maddalena. Signora, my youngest child, Maria. She speaks almost perfect English," he went on proudly. "Someday she will be a translator. She will maybe work at the United Nations.

Like you, she wants to make everyone friends in the world. Signora, I invite you into my home to meet my family." He gestured up the stairs.

Ashamed of her fears and suspicions, Maddy bestowed her brightest smile. "I am truly honored, Signore Bondini." Her steps light, she followed Maria up the narrow stairs. Indeed, she was delighted; she was to see a glimpse of Venetian life that no tour guide ever offered. And after this visit Bondini would take her to see the most important sight in Venice.

On the third floor a door stood open. A tall, slender woman with gray hair, dressed in an embroidered blouse and maroon skirt, stood there with her hands outstretched in welcome. "Signora Maddalena," she said. Maddy couldn't understand the words that followed, but there was no mistaking their intent.

"My mother says it is a great honor to have you here," Maria said, obviously proud of her ability to translate.

"Please tell her I am honored to be here."

Following the Bondinis into their apartment, Maddy saw a room flawlessly clean in the bright sunshine. Though the furniture had obviously seen much use, there were pristine lace antimacassars on every arm. Maddy remembered that there had been a lace-making school on Giudecca in the eighteenth century, and she made a comment to that effect. As Maria translated, Signora Bondini looked as though she might burst with pride.

Maddy gratefully accepted the offer of coffee and sat down in a green armchair that seemed strangely familiar. Of course! It listed thirty degrees to the left, just like the one in the living room at home.

With coffee—as strong and fragrant as the best coffee from the *caffès*—came warm panettone, a lemon-scented yeasty bread with chopped citron, nuts, and raisins. As Maddy was exclaiming over the bread, there was a merry hubbub from the hallway.

"My sons," Bondini said proudly. "The whole family comes on Sunday."

Suddenly the room was filled with handsome, energetic-looking young people, five gorgeous children, and a babe in arms.

"But you have twins!" Maddy exclaimed to Bondini's son Zorgi.

"Fraternal, just like mine!" Holding out her hands to the five-year-old boys, she explained to Maria that "fraternal" meant not identical.

The twins would not go to her, and their mother tried to urge them, but Maddy stopped her.

"I know what it's like. My girls went through that shy stage last year. Please don't make them feel uncomfortable. Maybe when they're a little bit used to me. But perhaps the baby would let me hold—him? Her?"

"Him," said Zorgi's wife, Luisa. "His name is Giovanni."

"Giovanni." Maddy smiled. "John. That was my husband's father's name. If we had a son, I think John would be his name."

If we had a son . . . The words ricocheted around her mind. A wild wind was pushing at the door that had long been closed.

Luisa Bondini lay Giovanni in Maddy's arms. His rosebud mouth trembled uncertainly, then broke into a great toothless smile.

"*Brava!*" the proud grandmother said, and Maria translated. "He does not let just anyone hold him, that one."

"Hello!" Maddy said, her face splitting in a grin that matched the baby's. "*Buon giorno.*" Holding him upright on her lap, with one hand supporting his neck, she said, "He's very alert. Look at those eyes. He's not missing a thing."

"And neither is the signora," Bondini said, his arms folded across the blue and white stripes of his chest.

Maddy looked at him; she looked around the room; she looked at the baby cooing in her lap. The reluctant door swung all the way open, never to be closed and locked again.

"You have certainly kept your promise," she said to him. "You have showed me the greatest treasure in Venice, the most beautiful sight in the world."

Chapter 12

I WANT TO HAVE A BABY," Maddy blurted out to Clark the moment she saw him.

They'd found each other at the aquarium in front of a tank where the whole undersea world seemed to be populated with polka-dotted creatures.

He looked at her in disbelief.

"I know it's a change," she said, her words tumbling one after the other, "but don't say no without hearing me out. I've waited this long to go back to college. I can wait a few years longer—until all the children are bigger and I really need a new life for my mind. Or maybe I'll never go. Maybe I have to live with the fact that I missed the moment. The girls' education means everything to me, but my own—well, there's plenty of time, and lots of ways to learn. So many ways to learn. But a baby—if we miss *that* moment, that's it. And I think it would be a mistake. A terrible, sad mistake."

He folded her into his arms, murmuring, "Maddy, Maddy."

"I think I felt it here the other day—the longing. Something about all these fish, the way the babies seem to happen while you watch. This place is just bursting with life. You could still go to college. I don't want you to think I'm backing out on the dream. We really don't have to worry about money now."

"We certainly don't," he said.

Something in his voice made her look up. The broad planes of his face were one big grin.

"What do you mean?"

"I didn't say no to Ian."

She shook her head in astonishment. "You didn't? But what about college?"

"The whole point of college was for us to have a chance to grow. To make us available to life's surprises. So what was I doing turning down this surprise? Besides"—he paused, the grin growing improbably merrier—"something had been nagging at me since I first came to the aquarium. It was the reason I brought you here yesterday. It made me—well, it made me want to propagate. But I wasn't sure it was something I could ask you. You know the chances are good we'll have twins again. And I thought you were so set on going back to college."

She buried her face against the sweet hardness of his chest. "Oh, heaven, I was drumming up all the enthusiasm I could muster. Because I thought you wanted to go back more than anything. You said yes to Ian. Truly? When do you start?"

"I didn't say yes. I just didn't say no. I told him I had to discuss it with you again before making my decision. But he knows."

"Everyone seems to know about us but us." She told him about her visit to the Bondini household.

"How remarkable. I envy you."

"Maybe we can visit again, together," she said.

He shook his head. "It seems wrong, somehow. It was one of those surprises you can't ask to happen twice."

Laughing, but serious, too, she said, "I almost have a feeling that if we went back those people wouldn't be there. As though they were actors who gathered today to give me to myself. Oh, that's impossibly narcissistic, isn't it? Of course they're real. They'd better be real. I have it all worked out, you see. Next summer Maria will come be our *au pair* girl. I'll need the help with the kids, and what could be better for her English?"

"That's right. Nellie and Kendra can teach her 'yuk' and other important words." He ruffled Maddy's hair. "I don't believe it," he said. "I just found another color. Burnt sienna. Lord, you're beautiful."

Nestling contentedly against him, she said, "If I am, it's because of you."

"Sweet liar. You even lie beautifully."

"Now, look here," she began indignantly. "Just because you're the official man of honor—How did you leave things with Ian, anyway?"

"He wondered if we'd fly down to Rome with him for a couple of days. In the Big Kangaroo. He'd like to take Donatello and Elena, too. And Elzbieta Cezeska. He wants to talk to someone in Rome about Donatello's tax problems."

"Why Elzbieta?"

"Why not? She's beautiful, she's exciting, she's good. We're not the only people allowed to be in love, you know."

"I had no idea!" Maddy exclaimed.

"Neither did I. Neither did he until this morning, apparently, when he woke up with her on his mind."

"Only on his mind?"

Clark playfully swatted her. "I'm glad you're so nonjudgmental, but let's not get carried away."

She pointed to the fish tank. "With what's going on in there, it's kind of hard to stay pure-minded. Are those two orange creatures doing what I think they're doing."

"And Mrs. Whelan gets an 'A' in biology. Let's go home and do some biology ourselves. After dropping your diaphragm in the Grand Canal."

"Clark Whelan! What an idea!" As they headed for the exit, she said, "So we hop on down to Rome. But we'll be back for the Redentore festival?"

"Absolutely. We can't miss that. Though fireworks in Venice seem almost like gilding the lily, doesn't it?"

She was silent for a moment. "We can't pretend any longer, you know . . . that our life isn't going to change."

"I don't think we have to pretend any longer." His hand on her waist was strong and eternal. "Because we know now that what matters will always stay the same. The rest is so many details."

"And what matters?" She knew, of course, but she wanted the ecstatic pleasure of hearing him say the words.

"CW loves MW."

"And MW loves CW," she chimed in softly.

"And CW and MW love KW and NW and LWTB."

"LWTB?" she echoed.

"Little Whelan-to-Be."

"Or Little Whelans-to-Be," she amended.

"However many, whatever flavor."

"You wouldn't mind another girl?"

"The world can always use another Ms. Whelan. Some good things you can't have too much of."

On which note they hurried to their hotel room.

Chapter 13

Iᴛ ᴡᴀs Aᴘʀɪʟ and rain was pouring down from the sky, soaking Honeydale.

As if on cue, Maddy's water broke. Though she'd been waiting for this signal for days, she was nearly overcome with excitement. Calling Clark on his private number, she imparted the thrilling news.

"I'll be home in twenty minutes," he told her. "Don't go anywhere. I love you, darling. Is there anything you need?"

"Just you. Drive carefully. Hurry, but not too much."

After calling her doctor and arranging to meet him at the hospital, she called Jill. "Can you pick the girls up at the bus stop? And bring them to the hospital? Oh, I wish Maria were here."

"We'll do fine until she comes," Jill said. They'd rehearsed this moment a hundred times. "And guess what, Maddy?"

"What?"

"The first of the Donatello baby clothes arrived today. I just knew it was a sign."

Maddy laughed with delight. "Well, thank heaven this is my last day for Donatello maternity clothes. Okay, hon. Got to go."

* * *

There was no problem picking a name for the boy: He was John. The girl was another matter. And then suddenly Maddy knew.

"Venice," she said to Clark. "Venice Whelan. So we never, ever forget."

"*The Banner* could run a name-the-baby contest," he teased.

"Don't you like the name? At least there won't be any others in her class."

Nellie and Kendra said they liked it. Jill said she liked it.

"I guess you won the contest," Clark said.

"But I can't sign an affy," Maddy said with a sigh, "since I'm related to the publisher."

"We'll find a loophole," Clark said. "I think I'm starting to like the name. I certainly like her. And him. And you."

Maddy's labor had been easy; the babies were beautifully healthy. Her obstetrician and pediatrician went along with her request for an early discharge. Twenty-four hours after Venice and John came into the world, Clark was bringing them and their mother home through the rain.

As they rolled effortlessly up their smooth driveway, Maddy commented, "Change is really not a bad thing. I confess I don't miss our potholes."

"In that case," Clark said, "maybe you won't argue with this." He got an umbrella out from behind the driver's seat, opened it, and came around to Maddy's side.

Carrying her two precious bundles, she docilely allowed Clark to shelter them all from the wetness. Inside, she nursed the babies, changed them, tucked them into their cribs, and checked on the presents she'd prepared ahead of time for the two big sisters. Then, to celebrate her happiness, her feeling of being one with the romance of it all, she ran out into the warm and gentle rain and got her hair soaking wet.

www.ingramcontent.com/pod-product-compliance
Lightning Source LLC
Chambersburg PA
CBHW022032170626
46808CB00003B/1168